HOU TALK TO BLACK PEOPLE

DEAR READER:

*T*he book you're about to read isn't easy. It's not fun. And while this is fiction, much of these pages are rooted in reality: a reality I wish we weren't writing about in 2019.

Instead of a dedication, I wanted to write a note to you

I was inspired to write this book in February of 2018. The story flew out in only two weeks, although different variations had been floating through my mind for months. After logging in to Facebook, I saw a friend post a video of her seven-year-old child cracking a pretty racist joke. The family sat around laughing, the mother put up a disclaimer that "They aren't racist, but this was funny because they don't know where she learned this joke," and it proceeded to rack up likes.

I was shocked, at first. But then I really started paying attention to my timeline. I went through my high school yearbooks – a very nondiverse, small town school full of rich parents and entitled children. I combined every thing I saw in conversations about race, racist memes, racist jokes, etc, into the creation of my main character, Ivy. Everything she says or does has been taken directly from my Facebook timeline since February of 2018. Even during the final edits, I chose to insert some harsh jokes in to her mother's dialogue based on my timeline feed.

I wrote this book because while I am tired of the "white person suddenly understands privilege" trope, I felt something was missing. I felt other books written to encourage people to explore their inherent bias and prejudice missed reality. They're sugar coated. They're dumbed down. They're written to make certain readers feel good. This is not that book.

Ivy is a very hard person to like. She's naïve. She's ignorant. She has no understanding that the world exists outside of her small world, and she mimics much of what we see today in the news, on social media, and in our friends and family. She's been taught how to view the world by her community, and this is something we need to work at. Almost immediately, you're not going to like her, but she exists here in my fictional world, and in many other real worlds. You may even know your own Ivy.

Without a doubt, I think you'll be frustrated with Ivy. I was briefly working with a publishing professional who, in order to further this book, wanted me to tone her down, to make her more likeable, and more apologetic for her actions. But that's not reality and I don't believe we should tone down the meat of a story so readers can feel safe instead of being encouraged to examine their own actions. We can't continue to lighten our fiction so people don't feel guilty, or lighten serious problems so they seem like an easy fix. If I had chosen to tone Ivy down, I might as well have thrown this book away.

I wanted to write a book that encouraged the reader to explore where they learned about race, how they're talking to their children or other people in their life about diversity, and how to take charge of their own education without leaning on the emotional outpouring of marginalized people. I didn't want to write a weak marginalized character who has to dumb down their life, although at some times, Alex, chooses to do so. Other times, he's raw and unforgiving. I feel like too often we rely on people from marginalized communities to hold our hands on our path to education without understanding the toll we take on their daily lives.

And I have seen too often, myself included, when we start to become aware, where we once again take ownership of marginalized people by speaking over them and taking away their agency. Because of this, I wrote this story from one point of view only, Ivy's. And while I do have diverse characters, I do not attempt to write from their point of view or tell their story. Although if you are a person of color reading this and you want to tell the story of Alex, his mother, or his father, I would love you to do so.

These pages were passed by a number of beta readers of different ethnicities. I even passed it through some of the people who inspired this book. I noticed my marginalized readers related to events where they've experienced what Ivy says or does. Many remarked she was silly, corny, or so stereotypical, but, also said they encounter these statements or jokes frequently. They simply choose to laugh it off because what else can they do? Some of my white readers wanted me to town down her actions because they could sometimes come off as harsh and shameful. They didn't want to be represented by someone like her when we shouldn't be having this conversation. They were right – we shouldn't be having this conversation in 2019. My hometown readers thought I was crossing a line and people just need to take a joke, everyone is too serious and gets too upset over nothing. One even told me racism isn't an issue because the "little Indian guy at the gas station smiles at her every day and she smiles back," when she buys her coffee. I hope they see this book everywhere and get really annoyed that people are having conversations about how they are growing, teaching, or recognizing their role.

I decided to publish *How to Talk to Black People* anonymously because I don't want the conversation to be about me as an author. I want the conversation to be about the social issues involved. This book not only deals with racism, but also class structure, the role of poverty in majority demographics against race, education systems, and more. I decided to make Ivy poor and struggling and to make Alex's family wealthy and highly educated. I hope to open discussions based on class and where we place people of color within our communities.

If you love this book, hate this book, or want to have a

discussion about what you've read, please feel free to email me: htttbp@gmail.com.

Finally, I want to thank everyone who worked with me on this book, read, edited, helped me research, told me about their experiences, and encouraged me to publish. I also want to thank the agent who finally dropped it because I wouldn't lighten up the hard scenes to secure the mass market. Because of these people, I'm able to put this book out into the world as I believe it's meant to be.

CHAPTER ONE

*I*vy stood between the elaborate mahogany doors, marveling at the silence of the grieving funeral attendees. They walked in groups, arms around each other, heads down, silent tears dripping on to the horrendously patterned carpet that made her as nauseous as the funeral itself. The urge to scream at them to cry, or sob, or make some sort of noise to indicate they were also in pain was threatening her sanity. At the same time, she was silently urging herself to be strong and hold her own grief together, to wrap her pain into a small ball and swallow the foul tasting lump, letting her stomach angrily digest the sadness until it passed from her body.

The idea she was even standing here, in the entryway to a viewing, was beyond her scope of comprehension. In a matter of days, she went from laughing and sharing deep conversations about life with one of her best friends to standing in this doorway, frozen, unable to move forward. At the end of the aisle spreading out before her, clogged with people whispering, patting each other on the back, and sharing sentiments of, "Yes, it's just awful," she knew his body lay in the casket. He was barely visible through the throngs of fake grievers who showed up with the express purpose of being seen. Nothing earns one brownie points like attending the city's highest-profile funeral.

She wished someone was there to hug her, to tell her

everything would be okay, that she'd recover from the pain of losing one of her best friends. But instead of support, she'd found notes in her locker blaming her for his death, emails telling her she should die, tagged in tweets saying it should have been her, and mentioned in Facebook posts saying her time would come. Notes trickled in from people who didn't even know him, who weren't friends with the precious soul lying lifeless in an oak box, soon to be dropped six feet under the ground.

Twenty feet away lay someone she would forever call one of her best friends. This room held her last chance to see him, to talk to him, and if she was brave enough, to touch him once more. She wanted nothing more than to walk up to the casket, slip her hand into his, and feel warmth creep back into his body. She wanted him to breathe again; his heart to beat again. She wanted to watch him climb out of the casket, look her in the eyes and tell her everything was going to be okay.

Unable to take even the smallest step forward, knowing that once she breached the threshold and moved from the doorway, she would be unable to turn back. She stood firm. Her legs planted themselves to the ground; her feet sowed seeping roots of pain into the floor. Warm bodies shuffled past, some even bumping against her unapologetically, but not one person stopped to talk to her or offer a hand to help her take baby steps forward.

Not one.

The attendees ebbed and flowed, moving in schools, working like magnets as they all pulled together; drawn to different groups of mourners they felt the need to console. Ivy scanned the room and saw his parents seated in the front. The crowds didn't notice them, and while some people would say this was because they knew his parents needed to mourn, Ivy knew otherwise. Talking to his parents would be out of their comfort zone. They'd have to break their judgment, rebel against the statement the cops released and the subsequent press conferences carefully staged on the steps of City Hall.

Acknowledging his parents meant they found truth in his mother's statement; the ultimate small-town betrayal. They'd have to pick sides: the town authorities or his parents. Even after the evidence was released, even after the truth was set free, the town chose quiet and safety over truth. And yet, even after making that choice, here they were, hugging each other, crying on each other's shoulders, patting each other on the back, and clearing their conscience so they could sleep easier at night.

His mother would never get to sleep easier. His father wouldn't get to sleep easier. Ivy's best friend Magnus wouldn't get to sleep easier. And it would be a long time before Ivy got to sleep at all, let alone easier. Even though people blamed her, even though people pointed fingers and left her notes, even though they cried their fake tears while talking about what they really thought behind closed doors, they still showed up here today ¬¬- a last minute social opportunity in a town obsessed with outward appearances.

Ivy knew the next week would be whispers about who didn't attend the funeral, what so-and-so wore, and how touched they were by a life tragically cut short. The life they didn't really know, but in this moment of self-repair, claimed for their own.

She felt the warm bile rise in her throat at the sight of Principal Penny standing near the front, hands tightly clasping other hands and issuing quiet condolences. He was busy hugging students, issuing words of safety and security to their parents, letting them know this was a rare event, and they shouldn't have to worry about their child.

Ivy knew what he was saying to them in between his words that sounded so politically correct: Don't worry. YOUR child is safe. YOUR child is a part of OUR world, and this won't happen to them. Principal Penny stood to the side of the casket, at the edge of the front row of chairs, like the official greeter for the season's hottest pop-up event. This wasn't his child; those weren't his apologies, or condolences, or comforting words to be taken and shared.

After shaking Principal Penny's hands, the flow moved to the front row – but not to his parents, to the Super Six. Even from the back, you couldn't ignore them. Their hair was perfect and not a single shiny strand fell out of place. Their outfits were perfectly selected: black sheath dresses made of thick, expensive cotton; form fitting but modest. Even their tears were majestic and manicured. The large diamond droplets that fell from the corners of their waterproof lined eyes would slowly run down their cheeks, perfectly rounded, and reflect every beam of light like a meticulously cut Swarovski crystal.

Fury shook her rooted frame. How dare those girls sit in the front row and make a claim to the pain his death has caused. People were hugging and apologizing to the girls for their loss while only giving his parents a glance and slight greeting. Ivy realized her community wasn't even able to comfort those they considered outsiders in a time of need and great pain. Even being educated and wealthy wasn't enough when they possessed extra melanin.

And yet while she stood here, judging the room full of her peers, their parents, and community influencers, she couldn't will herself to take one step forward. She couldn't push herself to move to the front, to demand the Super Six move, and embrace his mother. She couldn't bring herself to question the need for added security and a police presence in the parking lot. They should just let him spend his last days on top of the earth in quiet peace. And in the quiet buzz of the room, and the louder buzz of her mind, she couldn't even bring herself to say his name, to talk about him, or to talk to his memory.

She was struggling. The two remaining people in her life weren't here. Her mom couldn't take off work and Magnus didn't have the strength to attend another funeral tied to that house. And while she had convinced herself she was strong and able, and she needed to do this, and she needed to tell him goodbye and tell his parents she was sorry, and to convince herself that she was not the one to blame for his death, she realized she was wrong.

The burning sensation of hot liquid grew in her throat, pushing against Ivy's interior. The roots binding her in place broke, but she didn't move forward. Her first step was backward, away from the door, away from his casket, away from his mother's knowing eyes that had just looked over her shoulder and noticed her quaking form caught in the doorway. Her second step was more substantial, pushing her further away from the bullet-ridden body of the friend that saved her a few days ago. The body she wasn't there to save. The body that wouldn't have needed saving if it wasn't for her in the first place. Her third step was quicker, pushing her towards the large glass doors and freeing her from the overwhelming smell of carnations, rare tropical flowers, and dry, crinkly ribbons coated with chemicals. Her fourth step pushed her away from the somber music pounding its fists of anguish deep into her heart; the music he never would have wanted to be played at his funeral in the first place. The sixth step pushed her away from those people. The seventh and eighth step pushed her away from having to face her guilt. And the ninth and tenth step carried her outside, her body bursting through the double glass doors, knocking into people, ignoring their cries and scowls. She inhaled the fresh Midwestern air, letting the scent of freshly cut grass and mulch inject itself into her lungs. Once the smell of funeral bouquets was replaced by living flowers, she doubled over, allowing the bile its chance at freedom just off the side of the main sidewalk, right on top of the freshly cut grass.

CHAPTER TWO

*I*vy smacked her alarm clock a bit heavier than she should have; sending the small wooden paneled vintage monstrosity clattering to the floor. The noise echoed through her tiny over-stuffed room. She always wondered how such a small item could make so much sound. The clock's jarring roar seemed to reflect off every surface until each squawk successfully bounced around her and touched every single piece of anything carefully placed in the tiny box.

Today was the first day of school. Her body remained numb in her thin cotton sheets; her limbs still sleeping while her mind tried to furiously rouse them. Now that she was entering her sophomore year, she wanted to quietly fade into the walls and not have a repeat of the tragedy known as her Freshman year. She hoped she wouldn't be shoved into lockers or have to deal with the rich kids throwing trash at her when the teachers weren't paying attention. Growing up in Friendly Village was a challenge in itself; no one liked to be 'Trailer Trash.' And if there's one thing Ivy had learned, even if you do your best to look put together with clean clothes, clean hair, and clean shoes, people always knew you came from the court.

Society taught Ivy that once people knew you were poor, their mindset equated everything about you to poor. She was of above average intelligence but was often passed over when kids picked their partners. She was ignored for school contests, denied admission to advanced classes, and not accepted into newspaper, yearbook, or drama club. She tried to justify her rejections by telling herself she just wasn't as talented as the rest of her peers, but deep down she knew the student body who ran the organizations or influenced the teachers to accept certain people simply viewed her as a smudge on their journey to perfection. Ivy realized you could write circles around others, take better photos, paint better backdrops, solve Chemistry problems quicker, or memorize more Shakespearean dramas, but if you didn't have the social quota the queen bee's craved, you might as well keep to yourself.

The realization was making her lazy. She started a YouTube channel for her paintings, but once she tweeted a link to a video and the popular kids found their way over, the comments sent her into a depressed tailspin. The result was a quick shuttering of her YouTube, and her Twitter, followed by a caution from her guidance counselor that she needed to be tougher in the face of adversity or she'd never make it in this cruel world. Even those who were supposed to give teenage kids hope were locked up in the cycle of desperately seeking approval from only a core group of students while perpetuating the myth that specific demographics were useless. She tried to argue that the captain of the football team had no right to publically assume her deep-throating skills were directly related to the length of the brush handle she painted with, because this clearly made no sense, but she was quickly told to quit blowing things out of proportion.

The whole world ran on proportions, and the only way to truly make it one painful day past another painful day was to be the one setting the ratios. If life was a grocery store, she was the shopping in the bargain aisle of bulk tubes stuffed full of life's options, squeezing out just enough to fill her bag from whatever selections were on sale. Every day, life proved to her she was helpless, and hopeless, and would forever be a chained to someone else's definition of what she deserved to access. This week, life may give her lima beans and a surprise opening in the chess club. Next week, maybe Brussels sprouts and a window seat on the bus. Usually, it was kidney beans and a dry napkin thrown at her during lunch hour instead of a wet one.

The tingling in her legs and feet meant her body was beginning to wake up and she stretched gingerly, not filled with excitement but also not entirely filled with dread for the upcoming school day. The stillness of the double-wide trailer meant her mother was still sleeping, although her snoring wasn't audible, and she was likely going to wake up soon. Now that she was off the night shift and working a later afternoon slot at Pancake Palace, her demeanor was slightly friendlier. Ivy started to feel like less of a burden and possibly, a daughter again. Still, she didn't want to be present when her mom first woke up. She knew better than to be around before at least two cups of coffee and three cigarettes were ingested.

Ivy let out a giant yawn and debated whether taking a morning shower would be worth the risk of raising the motherly beast. She showered yesterday and didn't do any heavy physical activity. By all standard logic, she should be okay on the scent end of this debate, even though the personal hygiene side might want to put up a fight. She quickly sniffed each armpit and shrugged in approval.

"Nothing another layer of deodorant and a quick spritz can't hide," she whispered.

Even though reality continually made its expectations abundantly clear, and even if she may be moving more towards the lazy wallflower side of the high school demographic, Ivy refused to completely give up. She managed to book a slot at the local hair school as an end of semester hair model. This time, she was lucky enough to get a beautifully layered mid-length cut with a chocolate and copper balayage that set her golden eyes a flame; a huge sigh of relief after her last experience left her with a fire inspired dye job over an asymmetrical mullet. That was definitely a painful way to return to school after Spring Break and resulted in many hours spent on YouTube watching tutorials for clever braiding techniques to cover up the monstrosity she would be tasked with growing out.

She brushed her hair before running a creaky old hair straightener over the ends, feeling small hairs snag and quickly pull out with an uncomfortable pinch when they got caught in the ill-produced metal ironing plates. She was careful to not move too much so the cracked cord wouldn't pop the exposed wires and blow a fuse, or worse, shock her for the millionth time. The shocks were getting progressively worse, and she knew it wouldn't be long before she'd have to go to the thrift store and hunt for another flat iron in decent shape.

Her clothing selection was small but defined. She knew every piece by heart, even the new red tag finds. Today called for impact, but not too much. She needed to look polished but not flashy, put together but not fake, within her lane but not too poor. One leg at a time, she slid on the spandex free, heavy denim Levi's she found for a steal at the charity shop. Next came a longer aqua tank top that fell down to her hips, making it impossible to fail the strict dress code put in place to target only the girls, and only the girls out of the top social circle. While she would get detention for wearing a knee-length dress, no one seemed to mind when Pixie Marrow wore a skirt so short you could read what day of the week was on her ironic underwear. Ivy finished her first-day outfit with a western inspired rug print sweater poncho and caramel brown booties from her latest clearance rack haul.

She looked in the mirror and felt good, damn good, considering she was pulling this outfit off for under $32. Always the eternal realist, Ivy knew she would never be considered classically beautiful, maybe not even trendy beautiful, and by all accounts, she was likely to be marked as plain. But, she was comfortable with herself, her curves that hit everywhere except where the boys wanted them, her odd tiger eyes that almost matched the same shade as the forbidden light brown M&M, and her ever-changing beauty school finals hair.

Changing her mind on her footwear, she quickly tied her beat up Chuck Taylors – the one piece to her wardrobe she would never change and dreaded replacing, and the only clothing item society didn't mind being a little scruffy. She bounded to the kitchen with a pep in her step, hoping the two boiled eggs she made last night were still tucked in the Tupperware container. The mustard yellow fridge creaked open to reveal a half-eaten slice of cheese in an open wrapper, 1/12 a bottle of ketchup, an empty gas station cup of soda with red lipstick on the straw, and one solo piece of dried out bread that could substitute for house building material.

"Looks like she hit the bar again after work," Ivy scoffed, feeling her stomach growl in anger. She knew it was too late to make a run to the convenience store; she'd miss the bus if she tried. By the time her bus pulled in to school, morning breakfast in the cafeteria would be over. Her first two classes banned food and drink, and this meant she wouldn't have a chance to eat until lunch at 12:45. She looked at the kitchen clock and saw it was 6:53. A little less than six hours before her lunch break, and almost eighteen hours since her last meal of half a can of spaghetti rings. She had no choice but to make it through

"You got a problem today, Ivy?" her mother rasped from behind her.

"Not at all, Mother. Not at all, especially not since you ate my breakfast, that I paid for from my savings, and left me with nothing on my first day of school."

She tried to contain her frustration but looking over her mother's smeared heavy black eyeliner, dry lips chapping with flakes of last night's lipstick, and hair resembling unbaled hay, she had to fight harder than she wished. She knew it was best to excuse herself from the situation as soon as possible and move on to the bus stop before her mom started making accusations of Ivy suddenly being too good for them. An argument she never understood. She didn't ask to grow up in this small Indiana town or to go to a school district where most of the monthly family incomes far outweighed their meager yearly earnings.

"I have to get to school. It'll be fine. I'll eat at lunch." She sighed and quickly exited the room, grabbing her black leather backpack and bounding out the door. Her backpack was one of the few expensive things she owned, possibly the only valuable thing, and the result of the only time she had ever won anything in her life. Coincidentally, she didn't actually win the backpack in last year's homecoming raffle, but the girl who did had stepped out to contemplate losing her virginity under the bleachers and missed her name being called. Ivy was the second choice, but she loved to carry that beautiful, smooth, deep inky leather that infused its woody scent into all of her notebooks.

Behind her, the morning beast muttered something Ivy knew was meant to be hurtful, spiteful, or to negatively engage her time. She refused to let the words sink into her head and instead turned them into an animated caricature of various punctuation symbols flowing in and out of the room in a furious search for someone else to annoy.

"Hey, girl," Magnus said, waiving a little too excitedly from the rusted, bent steel post that once held a stop sign full of b-b gun holes. Even though the sign was gone, the lone green pole still served as the bus stop for the poor kids.

Friendly Village didn't get the door-to-door service the wealthier neighborhoods would get this morning. The driver stuck on their route had no desire to curve through the small lanes and try to coax a bunch of future drop-outs and delinquents from their homes. Every time Ivy thought about this, her blood boiled. Sure, she didn't have to walk more than fifty feet from her front door to the signpost, but the school made every effort possible to showcase there were dividing lines, establishing the fact that some kids were better than others. They never hid the way poverty made the wealthy uncomfortable. Perhaps the kids she got on the bus with every morning would have a better chance if they weren't subconsciously taught they weren't as good as their peers.

"What's with those shoes?" Magnus continued with a roll of his eyes, assessing the bargain bin ensemble Ivy had so carefully crafted. "I thought you just bought new sneakers? White ones. And didn't you say you bought cute brown ankle boots?"

"Yes, sir! $3.24 on the clearance, clearance, clearance. But you can't start a new chapter with anything except your lucky Chucks."

"Yes, yes you can. And what's with that backpack?"

Ivy twerked her mouth up on the right, her lips tightly clenched and her eyes narrowing. She worked hard to serve her meanest look possible and draw the line of outfit advice at her cherished backpack.

Magnus giggled and rolled his eyes, dishing back the silent, "I thought there was hope for you, but I give up," advice that he so often gave out related to fashion.

Coincidentally, Magnus wasn't poor at all. His parents were extremely wealthy. When their private jet crashed killing them both, he inherited their vast fortune. The caveat was the money would be locked in a trust fund until he graduated college with at least a 3.8 and enrolled in a Master's program. His parents' house went to his grand-mother, who was quite satisfied living in her quaint trailer. Out of spite to fight the man and consumerism that built her daughter's fortune, she sold the family house and all of the belongings inside before donating every last penny to the SPCA. She claimed it was those damn sad dog commercials that pushed her to do it, but Magnus knew selling everything gave her the last word on her jealousy over her daughter's success. Magnus had been at a summer camp disguised as three months of adventure but was really for orphaned children living with family members who didn't know what to do with them when the sale happened. He came home to find he wouldn't have a dime to his name for at least eight more years and would be living with his grandmother in a trailer smaller than his previous bathroom.

Everything was gone: his game systems, his collection of limited edition Jordan's, his autographed sports memorabilia, and his mother's BMW M3 he hoped would be his when his sophomore year rolled around and he finally got his license. While he was frustrated at first, he realized if he played by the rules, he would be able to repurchase everything on his own. But if he didn't, he'd be stuck in that damn trailer park.

Magnus had never been like the other rich kids in terms of showing off his family blessings. He first met Ivy over a childhood summer when he stayed with his gran for two months. His parents were off building schools or hospitals or something like that in some far off place only rich people and locals could pronounce, and where even though the location is relatively poor, it sounds like a pile of gold when its name drips from their perfectly filled lips. Their friendship never waned, even when the other rich kids came calling and tried to claim him for their own. Magnus always felt they only wanted him for what he could give, and the tragic death of his parents proved this when their offers slowly dropped off at the same rate as his visible wealth.

"What's your first class?" Ivy asked, leaning gingerly against the green pole, already feeling the fatigue of hunger, imagining the fragrance of hot French fries with every gust of wind that crept past. "I have Geometry 1 with Mrs. Particopian. Math. First thing in the morning."

"She's a tough one. She would collect our homework before the starting bell even rang last year. That woman loves her pop quizzes, too. Good luck," he smirked. "I have AP Econ first and then Chem 2. Basically, I'll be learning how to fund everything I want to create to blow up the bull-shit."

"I wish I could take an AP class," Ivy sighed, kicking the dirt. She knew her chances of getting into college would be higher with some AP classes on her transcript, but she couldn't argue her way in, no matter how hard she tried.

"Yeah, that sucks," Magnus replied.

They'd had many conversations about how Ivy was always told she didn't enroll quickly enough, there weren't enough seats, the class roster had been reduced, or she'd been put on a waiting list. Even though kids inevitably dropped, slots from the waiting list never actually opened and they all knew this.

"Oh, hey. Gran baked some banana bread and quiche. I packed some for us, but I think we're going to have Fran again this year. You know how she gets about eating on the bus. Want a piece? You'll have to eat it here, though, to avoid the wrath of Franba the Hut."

Ivy laughed, grateful for this small blessing. She eagerly took the homemade goods, trying her best to eat like a lady and not a greedy bridge troll. "Oh my goodness. Your gran's quiche really is the best. I could eat a whole pie of this all by myself." She groaned.

"I could have her make you one today. She'd love it, actually," he offered.

"Oh, that'd be great, but you know she'd go to all that trouble, and the moment I turned my back, the drunk prin-cess would eat it up."

"Is that why you look so exhausted this morning? No breakfast?" Magnus asked. "Have you thought about stashing cereal bars or something in your room?"

"Why should I have to? It's not my fault my mom hogs the food. Sometimes I wonder if she throws it away or feeds it to the raccoons just to make sure I don't get anything," she whispered, savoring the last bite of the fluffy egg cake. "I don't understand how she can despise me so much. She's never even home to know me."

Magnus draped his arm over his best friend's shoulder, giving it a gentle rub that reiterated he would always be there for her no matter what. The two sat in silence, waiting for the big yellow steel horse to finally arrive and carry them off to the first day of their sophomore year.

CHAPTER THREE

*T*he enormous brick entryway of the high school opened into an expansive two-story atrium-like hallway. The morning sun eagerly dripped through the glass roof, warming students as they bustled to meet friends they hadn't seen all summer, overachievers running to get front row seats in class, and the senior boys grouped on the sides to analyze the incoming freshmen girls. Ivy and Magnus moved through the crowds with predatory ease, knowing where to side step, when to suck in, when to spin, and when to take a quick pause to let someone they didn't want to interact with move past. While Ivy had developed her skills for monitoring a room and moving to meet her personal needs from kindergarten, Magnus had only recently needed to embrace the challenge of avoidance, not just invisibility.

The duo twisted and turned down the long hallway, past boastful display cases full of trophies, award-winning artwork, and photographs of various teams eagerly handing over bragging rights to the school. Maple Creek High School was known statewide for being the best in almost every sport, international champions in show choir, the reigning national champion marching band, and toppling any other state high school's theater program, debate team, mathletes, and fine art programs. The school was fitted with everything: three pools, two gymnasiums, an Olympic quality weight room, a science wing that included top of the line classrooms with features for safe chemistry experiments, biological dissections, a greenhouse for horticulture and even a miniature Skylab for astronomy. There was a full pottery studio, a photography studio with a dark room, a painting lab, and a lab split between textile design and printmaking. That was all on the first floor, and there were two and a half more to go. Not a dime was spared in the continued evolution of the school's offerings.

The large heavy doors of the theater swung open, almost knocking Ivy to her feet. She gasped in unexpected frustration and found herself face to face with four unfamiliar middle-aged women with too much plastic surgery and very-expensive clothing. They slung empty cardboard boxes on their right hips, luxury car key chains precariously dangling from one finger, and Starbucks cups adorned with flashy pink lipstick in their left hands. The site of the perfectly presented middle-aged women capable of passing for college students summarized the town's unrealistic expectations to look, act, and shop in the exact same fashion as everyone else. And to never grow old.

Ivy didn't recognize any of these ladies, and by their glare, they only recognized her lower social standing. She broke eye contact and reminded herself to straighten up and walk tall. A quick glance into the auditorium filled every inch of her insignificant body with dread. Down the large aisles were numerous booths advertising various businesses and the stage was set for what looked to be a panel discussion. This couldn't be good.

"Do you know what lunch block you have yet?" Magnus interrupted, breaching the row of double doors four sets wide that opened into the main halls of the school and set them free from the human clutter of the atrium. "I think I'll have third block on white days, second on red days."

"I really hate block scheduling. You know? The concept does nothing to organize our equilibrium. I'm pretty sure I'm fourth both days. You know how it goes. The powers that be don't want the ruffians to destroy the cafeteria for all of the pretty people."

"I was a pretty person once." He playfully deep sighed.

"You're still pretty to me, my love. Now, shoo. I have to get to class, and you don't want to taint what little bit of a reputation you still have with my presence."

"Fuck reputation," he replied, perhaps a little too loudly. A prompt scolding from a passing guidance counselor settled with a thinly veiled threat to start the year off in detention and led him to apologetically slink away.

Ivy carried on towards the back stairwell, which would place her closest to her locker, and further away from the locker bay that held the jocks and princesses. The first day of class was enough pressure without immediately falling into a metal fence of hungry Venus flytraps. She had one goal this year: survive and avoid.

Locker 8211 called out, and she happily approached, her quiet place of safety and familiarity in the ever bustling and changing school. She often wondered if she could escape from her day by crawling inside the metal walls and disappearing until the final bell rang. Perhaps this was due to living most of her life in a bedroom that wasn't much larger than her locker, or maybe she just really, really, really loved the suffocating hug of a room too small for human habitation.

She twisted the worn black dial three times to the right out of habit until she once again landed on five. Two turns to the left to forty-one, and one turn back to the right for seventeen. She expected to open the door and be greeted by last year's die-cut cat stickers adorning the door and a few stray layers of glitter nail polish from one night when she missed the bus, and her mother wouldn't answer the phone. Eventually, she gave up and walked the six miles home, arriving just after eight, only to find her mother having a party with a very motley looking crew of coworkers, and had willfully ignored Ivy's plea to be picked up on the voicemail.

The thick silver latch that would release the thin metal door held firm. "That's odd," Ivy remarked, positive she had twisted the dial the correct number of times and to the exact numbers each rotation. She tried again; her concentration laser sharp and unbroken by the hustle flowing down the hallway behind her. Five. Two turns to the left to forty-one, and one turn to the right until she landed on seventeen. She pulled up once again on the silver latch only for the mechanism to stubbornly catch, not release.

"That's my locker, actually," a voice came from behind her. She turned to face a pock-marked boy with thick brown hair and awkward fitting clothes claiming ownership of her domain. The obvious freshman held up a small envelope with the school's insignia and removed a card from inside.

"Oh, I'm sorry. I thought this was still mine. Well, enjoy her, she's a good one," she replied and turned to move towards her first class.

The walk to class was another dance of remaining unseen, untouched, and nonexistent. Ivy's path of choice was always the darker hallways snaking around the outer edges of the building, avoiding mass crowds. Knowing the chaos of the first day downstairs, the relative emptiness of the third floor was welcomed. Students were too busy mingling like killer bees to be floating through the upper hallways, and she relished the relative silence on the way to Geometry.

"Good morning, Mrs. Particopian," she greeted, slipping into a middle seat. Her choice showed she wasn't going to be a suck-up, but also wasn't a slacker. Her goal, which she proudly defined before the first bell even rang, was to be polite and slide by until she collected her diploma and took whatever steps needed to move on with her life.

The first bell rang, indicating two minutes until class was set to begin. Not a single other student had yet to arrive.

"I don't know what it is about the first day," Mrs. Particopian spoke up, interrupting the awkward silence. "I never have students in their seats and ready for class, even though they've been in school at least eight years by the time they get to Geometry. Well, might as well get started. What's your name? Pick up your book from the back, and I'll get your new locker assignment."

"Ivy Adams," she replied, sliding towards the stack of thick navy blue textbooks and searching for the newest cover. A new looking cover meant the glossy interior pages might still carry that new book smell – the smell Ivy wished someone would hurry up and bottle already. "About the lockers, why are they moving them?"

"Moving them? You get a new locker every year. The school believes doing this breaks up cliques and forces students to socialize with new people," Mrs. Particopian sighed. "Of course, cliques are cliques, and all this does is jam up the hall and make me write tardy passes." She handed Ivy an envelope identical to the freshman she ran into only a few moments ago at her old locker, the old locker she wished she still had.

The glue holding the triangular flap to the envelope's body softly popped when Ivy's finger slid underneath. She wanted to rip the edges, tear the card out, and stare at her new locker, but she also wanted to appear unconcerned, laid back, and not a threat to the harmonious atmosphere every teacher desperately wished their class would maintain. Her hands shook as she slipped the card out and stared at the number.

"1234," she laughed. "Well, that seems lucky. Should be easy to remember."

With her new locker assignment firmly planted in place, she started to run over the map of the school to find its location. The first number was the quadrant. Number one meant this year's locker would be on the entirely other end of the school, but also closer to the parking lot. Coming in and out of school would be easy, but the rest of the day would rarely accommodate the time she would need to cross from the south end to the north end, and down three flights of stairs. Number two indicated the zone. If she were correct, her locker would be the 34th locker in the hallway running between the foreign language labs and the science wing.

"Bummer. I'm not taking any foreign language this year, and my only science class is the end of the day. This locker is worthless," she said, unfortunately out loud, while the second bell indicating students should be in their class rang out. The room was still empty, which she was thankful for since the filter on her thoughts was apparently broken.

"What's your number?" Mrs. Particopian asked.

"1234. First floor, the hallway between science and foreign languages."

"You're not on the first floor, you're on the main floor. I know - confusing. They tried to do this whole zone and quadrant setup, but twelve is the exception. Bottom floor lockers are actually 0123, for example."

"The...main floor? But there are only two locker bays on the main floor," she stammered. The main floor had the entrance to the cafeteria, the atrium, the art wing, the gymnasiums, library, administration offices, and two long corridors of core classes. With these rooms all located on this floor, administration and high traffic entrances, locker bays were about as useful as a ball of hair in a shower drain. The main floor held two bays: the jocks by the gym and the princesses by the library and core class corridor.

"You'll be fine," Mrs. Particopian reassured. "You won't be with the boys, thankfully. You'll be smack dab in the middle of the girl's bay. Really great locker location, actually."

Ivy sighed, thankful the rest of her classmates had begun to filter in and she wouldn't need to explain why this was in fact not the ideal locker for someone like her. She slipped her phone from her backpack, knowing today would be the only time a mobile in class might be even slightly accepted. Magnus had to hear this because if she didn't tell someone or let out her frustration, she might explode in her red melamine chair in the middle of geometry on the first day of school.

"You are the girl I've been looking for my entire life. Is this seat taken?" Magnus teased and slid a turquoise lunch tray loaded with square pizza and nacho cheese into the empty seat across from Ivy.

"Magnus!" she squealed, containing her desire to jump over the table and squeeze him. "I thought you had an earlier lunch?"

"Sadly, no. Fourth block is the worst lunch. Like, ever. You have to sit in class and smell all of the food, even if it's not that good. My stomach sounded like an overexcited baby humpback whale today. So embarrassing."

"At least today is pizza day, though! I really hope once we graduate there is some way or somewhere to buy these pizzas. They're the best," Ivy replied, greedily dipping her greasy rectangle into a healthy pool of bright red French dressing. "I mean, where do they get this stuff? Everything else they serve us is shit, except for this pizza."

"Pizza and the chicken sandwich that isn't made out of real chicken. Those are my mea culpa. So, about this locker drama. You're really in the bay of bitches?"

"I'm really in the bay of bitches... I'm seriously thinking about just carrying everything with me ... every day. Even if that means bringing a backpack and a messenger bag, breaking my back, and getting pit stains in my shirts. Magnus," she whined, "It's not fair. I know I'm no angel, but what did I do to deserve this?"

Magnus laughed, dropping his head into his hands. "Have you thought about the potential upside? Maybe you'll get a new best friend, a flashy ride to school, or a makeover like in the movies when the rich girls take on the down and out secretly hot chick."

"You're an asshole," she laughed, flicking a stray piece of lightly coated lettuce from her tray on to his shirt. "I'm not a secretly hot chick. If they gave me a makeover, I'd look the same, just more expensive."

"I may be an asshole, but you're a jerk," Magnus replied. He furiously dabbed the greasy orange blob that was not blending with the delicate blue stripes of his button-down shirt. "This is one of the last remaining shirts from my days as a rich kid. Well, was. I think this stain will set in before I get home."

Ivy stammered, running over all of the ways she should apologize. The shirt wasn't just a leftover piece of his previous wealth, but a piece of his parents. The cotton button down was a reminder of what life felt like when he was someone's son, when he came home to parents, and home cooked meals, and when his largest problem was a full DVR when he wanted to binge on Netflix instead of watching other programs. Ivy often fantasized about having decent parents, or how she would celebrate if something unbecoming happened to her mother that left her an orphan. She would never admit these feelings to Magnus. She couldn't. He would never understand why losing her mother, no matter how horrible she was, could ever be a fantasy after she already lost her dad.

Eventually, a soft apology slipped out. The square pizza lost its flavor, quickly moving from a welcomed wondrous stomach filler to a blob of grease flavored cardboard. Moving forward, the need to be observant and aware of every small piece of Magnus would be crucial. With new budgetary constrictions, his style had become more quirky, and definitely not as refined. The shirt he wore today must have cost at least $150 judging by the smooth cotton that had yet to fade, the way the shirt held a press for hours, and the bright contrast floral wrist cuff that offset the traditional button-down striped shirt.

"I'm sure Gran knows some way to pull this out. Did you know she puts hairspray on ink stains? I sat on a leaking ballpoint pen last week at bingo, ruining one of the only pairs of jeans I can currently find for these long legs that don't make me look like a stork. She sprayed them, let it dry, and the damn things washed clean."

"Fascinating. Listen, Magnus," she whispered. "I really am so, so, so sorry. Forgive me?"

"Don't be silly. Of course I do. This is just a shirt. Friendship can't be bought, or ruined by stray lettuce. Besides, you know too many of my dirty secrets. The price of this shirt is a small price to pay for your continued silence on many, many, many issues," he laughed and winked.

Ivy sighed, deep relief flooding over her and quickly turning her taste buds back on. She eagerly dipped into her pizza, eating the remaining half with fervor before the bell rang and dismissed the cafeteria. Unless she stumbled on some pocket change on the way home, this might also be her dinner.

"Did you see they're doing a career fair tomorrow? On the second day. And during our study hall periods. I really think they're out to kill us or figure out who they're willing to feed to the zombies first in the upcoming and inevitable apocalypse."

The revelation explained the trio that popped out from the auditorium in the morning. Ivy wondered if they were here to set up for their husband's business, if they were trying to convince girls they could be independent and economically sound if they only spent $599 to buy a start-up kit and sold make-up door to door, or if they were, in fact, independent business women capable of inspiring a room full of modern feminists who truly believed they could do anything. Ivy wanted to believe she could do anything, but she was part of the group where life was firm in not only its expectations but willingness to reach out and assist.

"It's so stupid they way they push their dreams on you

and then leave you out to burn," Ivy sighed. "I guess it's better now than midterms or finals."

"Who has the time, too? I just got my first essay in Classic Literature and a research paper. They take these AP courses very seriously," he laughed.

The impact of his words quickly settled over Ivy's face even though she tried to fight the oncoming scowl. She could see the apology forming in Magnus' light green eyes as he realized this time, he was the one who forgot the obvious pain point in their friendship.

In only a few short seconds, the tables had turned. Ivy started to tell him everything was okay, she knew he didn't mean it, and not to worry, but the lunch bell rang out, sending students scattering and scrambling towards their next class. She took this as the universe telling her to let the hurt sink in a little bit longer and quietly stood up, leaving her tray on the table, and exited the cafeteria. She didn't care about being invisible, untouched, or ignored this time. She barreled through the hallway on her way to Child Development, the class all students the school thought were high risk for pregnancy got funneled into under the guise of no other available health electives. The joke was on them, though. Ivy was a virgin and she sure as hell was not going to waste one second of time on any of the overinflated egotistical males around here.

CHAPTER FOUR

*I*vy sulked into the auditorium behind her classmates, hoping to do a ballerina worthy spin into a dark corner and avoid the next hour of overly energetic, information-heavy speeches from successful community members who made something out of their lives. There would be the typical doctor, lawyer, nurse, college professor, and pharmacist, but there would be no blue-collar jobs present. The Maple Creek school system made no effort to hide their bias towards continuing education, or their opinions on the social standing of those who chose to dirty their hands for work. One only learned to fix cars, pipes, food or hair if they had no other option, or, had failed at the life society wanted them to live.

Many times, Ivy wanted to argue that one could make a very respectable living and find enjoyment in industrial trades or service work. She learned her lesson last year when she used the example of her father. Even though he worked at the local automotive plant, he was able to bring home well over six figures each year, squirreling plenty away for future dreams, like buying a house and putting his daughter through college. The auditorium broke out in simultaneous laughter at the preposterous thought until one of the football players called out, "If your dad makes so much, why do you wear second-hand clothes?"

Ivy bit her tongue until her mouth tasted like a dirty

penny and her nerves picked up on the pain. Magnus had rested his hand on her quivering leg, trying his best to comfort her, and provide a reminder this was not her fight. The laughter grew. The echoes of hearty chuckles bounced over the ceiling and padded walls, landing on her heart with a heavy punch.

"He's dead, you fuckwad. An engineer requested him to fix a machine and forgot to turn the breaker off because his nose was stuck so high in the air he refused to look back down to earth. His educated royal highness made a mistake that crushed my dad in the door press and killed him. So screw your education and your ego," she screamed, silencing the room before running out, leaving everyone (including Magnus) stunned.

For her outburst, she was given one week of after-school detention. The other student didn't even get scolded. Not after publically insulting her, and not after laughter rang out again when she burst through the auditorium doors, heavily panting and desperate for fresh air that didn't settle with regret in her lungs.

Last year's career fair was the day she decided to be invisible and unseen; the year when the realities of the world broke her naïveté and her dreams. Her mind was no longer impressionable, no longer wet clay begging to be set. The memory of her dad, whom she had always remembered as a kind, loving, and hardworking man, was tarnished on the waves of mocking laughter.

An opportunity to duck away and avoid a repeat of last year never presented itself, and her only choice was to continue to shuffle in with the rest of the sophomore class. Her hands were tightly folded in her lap and her eyes locked tightly on the stage. She eyed the guests and tried to anticipate what each panel member would talk about, try to convince students they wanted to be when they grew up, or if they brought any cheesy key chains or lanyards with them to toss into the crowd, hoping they'd get cheers like a pop star. Luckily, the wide auditorium aisles had careful rows of career displays running down the center this year, providing some cover from the full group of rowdy students.

"Testing, testing..." Principal Penny recited into the silver microphone, tapping on the thin metal cage. A screeching thump erupted through the auditorium. "Welcome, sophomores! I'm so happy to have your attention today and welcome you to Maple Creek High School for another great academic year. I know I'm partial, but this year we have the best athletes, musicians, singers, and well, anything else that the great state of Indiana has ever seen!"

Cheers and whoops burst forth from the students who ate up every word about their inherent greatness. They wore their school name like a badge of honor and never hesitated to declare their excellence when face to face with someone from another district. The only school that could strike fear into the hearts of a Maple Creek Lumberjack was a Central Heights Saluki.

Principal Penny held his hands out towards the audience, patting the air to tell the room to settle down. The smile on his face betrayed his desire for calm and all too strongly supported how much he loved the power in his position. "There's no better way to encourage all of your fresh, young, eager minds quite like those who have been in your shoes before and persevered to greatness. The panel behind me consists of former Maple Creek graduates. These Lumberjacks kept working hard, long after leaving our halls, and have certainly made us proud! They've studied all over the country, and in some cases, all over the world, until they reached the pinnacle of success. Every person behind me has been nominated, for and most have won, prestigious industry awards, been in major national press, and worked with some of the brightest minds the world has ever seen. Together, they have a combined yearly salary of $89 million. Let me repeat that, kids. A yearly salary of $89 million."

The room gasped. Ivy could practically smell the spit forming rabid puddles of foam in the corners of mouths all around her. Most of the students were eating this drivel up, believing that one day they would be asked to return to this stage and brag about their own achievements. She, on the other hand, looked at the ten presenters on the stage who would drive her mad for the next ninety minutes and realized through the law of averages that each person made well over five million dollars a year. The concept of what someone could even do with that amount of money was utterly lost on her. She would consider herself rich at $50,000 per year, and well enough to take care of her needs and feed her mother if she was able to make just $18,000 a year. Some of these people made her financial goals in a week, maybe even a day.

Her eyes drifted over the room, taking in the look of delight and greed sparkling on the faces of her classmates. A few of them were so charged at the thought of making enough money to wipe their butts with dollar bills every day that lightning practically sizzled out of their heads.

"Madness, isn't it?" Magnus whispered into her ear from behind, causing her to startle.

Ugh, don't touch me," Jenna Goldman harshly whispered from her left, rolling her eyes when Ivy apologized as expected. She really wanted to tell her arch frienemy to shut up. Jenna's family was only one paycheck or one layoff away from joining the neighborhood in Friendly Village. Still, she wasn't poor trailer trash just yet, so she believed she had a leg up on a few people and took every opportunity to let it be known. Ivy had no doubt Jenna would one day be so desperate for acceptance and to climb the ladder that she would be willing to do whatever it took. And she did mean whatever it might take. She would probably then claim she was a feminist who climbed to success on hard work, when she had climbed to moderate success through bribes and sex.

Blowing off the deep disgruntled sigh from Jenna, Ivy turned in her seat, making no effort to avoid bumping into Jenna or respecting her space. "What are you doing here? I mean, how did you find me?"

"Luck, my dear, luck. They just can't keep us apart," he laughed. "No, in all seriousness, I asked Mrs. Furstenreider to let me sit behind you in case you had another outburst. No joke."

"Seriously? Why would you do that to me? I'm over that fiasco," she snarled, ignoring the grunts to her left.

"Hey, listen, I didn't get a chance to see you yesterday and apologize for lunch. Did you, um, miss the bus last night and today or did you find a ride?"

"I walked," she replied. Stubbornness was a quality she enjoyed. If she wanted to ignore Magnus, she would, by any means necessary. Truthfully, the situation wasn't so much about being hurt by his words and assumption as it was about taking the guilt off of her own shoulders for the dirty lettuce on the shirt. If she could make her friend feel guilty, it was like he absorbed her guilt and they could proceed, skipping down the Yellow Brick Road of dysfunction together, slaying demons along the way.

"Well, listen, I'm sorry. So, take the bus home with me tonight? Please? I had to sit next to Booger Barry. You should have seen the stringy slimer he knocked off into the window frame today. Please, don't make me sit through that again. I'm begging you," he pleaded.

Booger Barry was the worst. He had no manners, and the very idea he was raised by humans and not by a family of Silverback Gorillas baffled many. If he was so uncouth, perfectly fine with displaying all of his bodily functions, and apparently allergic to soap for both the body and clothes, what in the world were his parents like? Better yet, what would their house be like? The thought sent a shiver up her spine, and she agreed with a silent nod of the head to relieve Magnus from potentially becoming a human

Kleenex on the bus ride home today.

The first speaker was saying her farewells, blowing kisses to the crowd like a beauty queen. Ivy watched the presumptuous gesture and promised every cell in her body that when she did beat the odds, she would never treat a room full of strangers like an adoring crowd of puppies.

"Wonderful speech, Pamela!" Principal Penny clapped, making no effort to look at his students as the tall black stilettos carried Pamela away from the podium. "Well, that was certainly engaging. Wasn't it, sophomores? How many of you are now interested in industrial real estate?" The response was somber, mainly consisting of some wolf whistles from a few quickly shushed hormonal teen boys, and grumbles from girls mad their crush apparently liked older women with dresses too tight, boobs pushed too high, and hair too hair sprayed. Hair was made to move, not withstand gale force winds without budging, after all. "Next up is the world-renown neurologist and medical pioneer, Dr. Strafford. Let's give him a round of applause!"

The room was sent off in a frenzy. "Strafford," Ivy whispered. She nudged Jenny who tried her best to ignore the bump. "Is that Strafford as in Leslie Strafford?"

"Queen of the Super Six Leslie Strafford? Yes. You know, from the moment they moved here, every single mom has been trying to get their kid to be friends with her. Did you know her dad is single? Her mom died in some horrific ... oh, I'm so sorry," she grimaced.

"Not the same," Ivy snapped, dismayed at having to listen to public enemy number one's father speak about how great he is.

Dr. Strafford began his speech, speaking about how his excellent grades in high school gave him the freedom to pursue an academic scholarship. He wasn't athletic, he said, but his well-carved body said otherwise. Even in scrubs, everyone could see the lack of fat and precise sculpting of his muscles. The dreamy doctor successfully captivated the

entire room. The girls were drooling, the boys were idol-
izing, the remaining career day participants were deciding
if they should just pack up and fake an emergency to avoid
following next in line. He continued with the same advice
for taking an undergrad: work hard, avoid parties – this
drew a huge groan ¬¬– and get into the belief that you've
already been accepted into your medical college of choice.

"If you act like you're already there, you're more likely
to produce the quality of work they look for in incoming
medical candidates," he advised.

The handsome doctor scanned the room, preparing
to ask a question and make an example of a student. "You,
right here. Third row in the blue button-down," he called.
All heads turned to face the student who was the lucky
chosen one. A few gasps and a few mutters carried through
the auditorium. Ivy couldn't see the student fully, only a
fraction of the back of his head. She was caught off guard
by slightly thick, very dark hair, expertly cut to frame the
neckline of a dark-skinned teenager.

"Who is that?" Jenna gasped. "Is he … do we have a
black student now?"

"Maybe he's someone's assistant?" Ivy replied, just
as confused. "I've never seen him before. I haven't heard
anyone talking about a black student, either. Don't you think
we'd know? I mean, they'd probably make an announcement and put us through training," she laughed in time
with Jenna.

"What's your name?" Dr. Strafford asked the mysterious student.

"Alex," he replied, sending another round of hushed
whispers through the auditorium and settling the question
on whether or not he was a student or assistant.

"Great. Nice to meet you Alex. I'm sure you have big
aspirations for your life. Maybe you want to play ball and
dream of traveling the country in a private jet. But what
happens if you get hurt? What do you have to fall back on?"

"Those aren't exactly my plans," he started, interrupted by the doctor who didn't want to lose control of his discussion.

"Great. Let's talk about college. Don't you think your parents would be so proud of you if you went to college, let alone medical school?"

"Of course," he replied. "They'd be ecstatic."

"It's always great to be the first in your family to accomplish something, break some boundaries, and set your future family up for success. Ay, Alex? Wouldn't that be great to do something your parents may have only dreamt of?"

"Well, yeah. But, that'd be pretty hard in my case."

"I'm sure would be, Son. But, with enough hard work and dedication, you can get there. You're in one of the best schools in the country, and you can absolutely take advantage of some great opportunities to get into medical school," Dr. Strafford cheered.

"That's still not what I mean," Alex replied again, obvious annoyance layered over his voice.

"Don't give up so easily, Son. You don't have to fall into the same cycle as your parents. I'm sensing some hesitation. Let's work through this together. What would keep you from moving forward and breaking the expectations of your parents?"

Alex stirred in his seat, obviously uncomfortable. "You're Dr. Strafford...as in THE Dr. Strafford that was nominated for the Hugh McCreary Neuroscience Innovation Fellowship last year?" he asked.

Dr. Strafford straightened, pride showering over his face. "Yes. I'm surprised you've heard of the McCreary and me. It's normally only talked about in the inner circle," he said with air quotes. "Did you see me on local TV last year? I did give quite a few interviews on the news."

"No." Alex laughed and continued, "Not at all. As a matter of fact, I was at the awards banquet, cheering my mother on when she won the fellowship for her pioneering technique in micro-robotics for non-invasive hematoma and aneurysm treatment. If I can recall properly, you were nominated for completing someone else's previous procedure slightly quicker?"

A hush fell over the room and Dr. Strafford straightened himself. "Your mother is Dr. Trowler?" he asked, receiving only a nod from the student he had tried to isolate only moments before. "Well, she is an amazing woman and a fantastic doctor. Absolutely groundbreaking in her research. You do have some very tough shoes to fill." He nervously laughed. "So, um, anyone else in the room have any questions for me or need help clearing any objections as to how you could one day be a successful doctor?"

No one raised their hand. All eyes were tightly locked on the new student.

"Did you see that? Or better yet, hear that?" Magnus chirped through the crowd of bustling students pushing towards their next class. "Who was that kid?"

"Well, obviously some famous doctor's son, which means he's out of our friendship league," Ivy replied.

"Speaking of those who are out of our league, have you been to your locker yet? Did you get attacked by wolves?" he mimed, throwing his hands in the air and growling like an angry dog.

"Absolutely not. I just can't do it, Mags. I think I'm going to have to carry my books with me all day or take a bathroom pass during class to make a locker run. I mean, just the thought of being in that bay is beyond unbelievable. I can't believe they would do that to me," she whined, slumping her shoulders and kicking imaginary pebbles down the hallway.

"Everything challenges your will to live," Magnus whispered loudly. "I mean, it's just the way we get to experience life, isn't it?" he quickly spat.

Ivy glared. "So I'll see you after this class, and we'll walk to the bus together? I have Pre-Chem. Where are you?"

"Chem 2," he replied.

"Great. We're close by. We can just walk down the middle of the hallway, and when we run into each other, that's our meeting spot," she cheered, returning to her usual energetic self – the side she buried over the last year and strongly willed to die.

Ivy slipped into Pre-Chem, picking an aisle row. The stairs outside of the science hall would lead directly upstairs and come out in the hallway facing her locker. If she had to make a mid-class locker run, this would be the course. Of course, making a locker run in the last period of the day didn't make a whole lot of sense. She'd be better off just leaving her books at home and carrying what she needed each day. Students in her levels never had large projects, huge papers, or excess research material. The teachers knew better than to waste their time or effort, and they knew they wouldn't be winning any teacher of the year awards or have any movies made about them from leading these kids. They weren't bad enough to be noteworthy, and not interesting enough to occupy too much time.

The final bell rang to another half empty class. Ivy eyed her teacher, trying to get a read on Mr. Green. He had a post-military high and tight but the stomach of someone who loved donuts, dozens of doughnuts. His plaid shirt and olive green pleated pants said he shopped for himself, but the tight ironing and front creases indicated he had a wife who followed a specific routine. No dry cleaner willfully put front creases into pants now that the nineties were over, and no man could iron that precisely. He stayed behind the tall black granite countertop that served as his experiment and instruction station, reading the Wall Street Journal, and patiently waiting for the rest of his students to filter into the room.

After six minutes had passed and only one desk was

left, Mr. Green cleared his throat and stood to his feet with a screeching of his metal stool when it slid over the linoleum floor. "Welcome to Advanced Chemistry 3," he cheered in a deep boastful voice.

A chorus of groans, gasps, and shuffling of papers to check schedules tore through the silence. Ivy felt her heart drop to her feet. If she accidentally sat in the wrong class, that meant she would have to get up, leave this room, and enter another room. Science teachers were notorious for being strict and orderly due to the experiments and tools they had to supervise. Being late to a science class was an absolute guarantee for detention. During the first week, teachers allowed for some leeway, but they wouldn't allow for ten minutes.

"Just kidding, kiddos," Mr. Green chuckled. "You're in starter Chemistry. This class is like getting a chem kit for kids for Christmas. We're going to have a fun year, make some things blow up, catch fire, disintegrate in acid, and hopefully, not hurt anyone or ourselves in the process. Now –" he was interrupted by the door opening and turned with an eyebrow raised. "Well, thank you for showing up," he said to the student who entered past the acceptable time frame.

"I apologize, Mr. Green," Alex replied. "I'm still getting used to this school's layout. I wanted AP Chem. You know, college. My guidance counselor said that class was full, though."

"Interesting, Newbie. Welcome. Take that seat there," he pointed, directing Alex to an empty desk in the middle of the front row. "AP Chem, huh? But you're stuck here with us in kiddie chem."

"Looks that way. I took Intro to Chem in sixth grade. I've taken four other classes since then, but the school won't take the credits. Said something about me being too young to possibly be able to understand complex science."

"Wow, a big shot among us. Do you want to come teach

the class," Mr. Green boasted.

"His mom's a big-time doctor," a girl's voice from the back of the class rang out. "You should have heard him shut down Leslie Strafford's dad at the career fair."

"Well, I'm just yanking your chain, Alex. It's great to have you here with us. If you can't get moved up, I hope other students will consider asking you for advice when they think they're too good to ask me, their oh so humble teacher of the subject they will inevitably fail due to pride alone. Now, as I was about to say before Hotshot joined us, tardies are not tolerated in this class from this day forward. We run a tight ship here. We'll be using chemicals, fire, glass, cool things that may break, burn, or explode. We need you to be on time and paying attention to every single move you are making with these items. Anyone who comes late will be sent to detention, no questions asked. And of course, you know that means if you get too many day detentions you will have to repeat the class or ruin your summer by spending it with me again. I can already tell I don't like any of you enough to waste my summer spending it with you. Now, we're going to go right into the good stuff and learn about chemical reactions. One at a time, come up to the front and grab a ping pong ball from the bucket." He paused, waiting for students to move and follow his clear, easy to follow instructions. "Well, okay then. Too cool to even make the first move. This side," he said, pointing to the left row of desks, "starting in the front to the back, one at a time, then each row follow suit. Let's go!"

The students did as they were told and moved into position, grabbing their ping-pong balls with sticker numbers and sitting back at their desks. Ivy looked at her small sphere, running her finger over the number eleven, her lucky number. A tiny sliver of happiness settled over the discovery, and she took this as a sign her dad was looking over her shoulder, telling her everything would be okay. She wasn't religious, didn't hold any esoteric beliefs, but every now and then she would smell her dad's cheap woody cologne on a breeze or in a room when she was feeling lonely. When she was overcome with anxiety and fear, or if she had to make a choice, somehow, the number eleven always showed itself.

"Good work. Your first exercise in following instructions has been completed. If you can successfully execute those steps, you can successfully complete the next experiment. All you have to do is read this paper and follow the very simple English instructions. Please follow each number exactly as written. Now, for your lab partners." He paused, interrupted by the quickly erupting chatter and quick movement of students popping up to move towards their friends. "Back to your seats," he belted. "You must be mad if you think I'm going to let you pick who you want to do this with. We need order and focus, not chatter and gossip. Pick up your ping-pong ball and find your match, then come up to the front, drop your balls back in the bucket, and grab an instruction sheet. Next, move to the lab station that coordinates with your number. This will be your partner for the rest of the year. Your grade will rely on the ability for this person to follow instructions, focus, and get to class on time. If your partner turns out to be an absolute waste of time and space, come talk to me around midterms, but not before. Okay, class, break!"

Madness ensued. Students called out their numbers like a thirty person live auction, stepping over desks, clogging up aisles, and kicking over book bags to find their partners.

Ivy rolled her eyes and sighed. She didn't want to participate in the madness, and no one had screamed number eleven yet. Deep down, she hoped this meant there was no one else with a number eleven and she could finish this year's work on her own. Picking up her notebook and blue ink pen, she plodded towards workstation eleven and scooted on to her stool. She would patiently wait until the madness calmed and one student was left, or hopefully, that student was also smart enough to avoid the madness and just head back to their workstation.

"Number eleven? I think we're partners."

The voice broke her deep concentration on notebook doodles. She laid down her pen, took a deep breath, and prepared herself for the worst. She debated on the best response but also knew snark or sweetness would depend on who was behind the voice. She raised her eyes from her pen sketches and gasped as she focused on Alex.

"Yeah, this is number eleven," she stammered. "I'll take our ping pong balls back up and grab the instructions." Shaking, and hoping the tremor wasn't obvious, she laid her hand out for him to place the ball in her palm. "Seriously, it's okay. I can take them back up," she asserted, slightly annoyed he didn't trust her with a stupid ping-pong ball.

Too annoyed to worry about decency or first impressions, she snatched the opaque white sphere from his hand, double checked the sticker said eleven, then tromped to the front of the class. She gingerly dropped the balls into the bucket, snatched two instruction sheets and swiveled on her heels with the precision of a majorette.

"You and your partner get bonus points," Mr. Green said, just loud enough to get her attention but not loud enough to be heard by everyone still jumping over stools like uncaged zoo animals.

"We do?" She spun back around, shocked to be acknowledged and suspicious of a change in her cursed high school fate.

"I like to see how people work. I should have been an anthropologist instead of a chemist. Anyway, each year, I give bonus points to the first partners who make their life easier and show independent thinking. Shows me you're serious and can problem solve. These are good traits for a future scientist! What's your name?"

"Ivy. Like the plant," she nervously laughed.

"That's not the worst name I've heard. And you're with

Hotshot. Gotcha. That's fifty extra bonus points for both of you. Enjoy your first experiment!"

Stunned and bewildered, she took a wide sliding side step towards her partner while keeping a side eye on her teacher. She tried to read his face for a hidden agenda but came up empty. "Okay, then," she said, taking another wide sliding step towards the rear lab tables. "Thank you for that." A small spring bounced into her step from the secret gift. Perhaps this would be the year her life started to change, and good things came her way.

"Looks like we're going to be dissolving Tylenol," she said, slipping back on to her stool and handing Alex his copy of the instructions. She was confused by where the possible excitement or danger could be in this experiment. "This sounds so boring. We're going to drop some Tylenol into a cup of saltwater, distilled water, vinegar, and cola.

"Of course we are. We need to create a hypothesis first and note our control. I'm going to presume based on what I know that the acid and sugar content of the cola will dissolve the Tylenol the quickest. What do you think?"

"I think your instructions are basic and common sense for anyone old enough to have done a basic experiment," she snapped.

"Well, okay. Let's get going," Alex replied with a smile. He opened the small cabinet door under the lab station and removed four red solo cups, four labeled bottles of liquids, and a small bottle of acetaminophen. "Okay, first things first. We need to set our control. Through the bottle, all of these feel room temperature to me. What do you think?" he asked, tipping the premeasured liquids into individual cups.

Ivy stuck a finger into the first cup, the cola. "Feels pretty room temperature to me. It's awfully fizzy." She quickly moved to stick her finger in the next cup, the vinegar.

"Stop!" Alex commanded before he let out a soft laugh. "Sorry, didn't mean to make you jump. You can't do that.

You'll have residue from the cola on your finger, and you'll contaminate the vinegar sample. If this were a lab, the sample would be ruined, and the experiment would possibly be over. Truthfully, we shouldn't use the cola now, either, but it's not that deep. I won't tell if you won't tell."

"A control? Look around you at this room. Do you think a control or baseline matters? Your powers of observation need serious assistance." Picking up her pen to take notes, she tucked her head to hide the burning red heat creeping up her cheeks. "I should write this down, yeah? Four red cups ... do you think the size matters? My limited experience says it doesn't."

"If you're talking about the experiment, absolutely. Let's see, the bottles are marked for eight ounces, so the cup must be 16 fluid ounces."

She felt foolish; her joke falling on deaf ears. She'd have to try harder. A fool's stroke of luck paired her with quite possibly the smartest boy in school. She needed him to see value in their partnership, maybe even open doors for friendship. "Oh, by the way, we were given fifty extra bonus points for being the first partners to meet at their table instead of acting like wild animals. Pretty cool, huh?"

"Yeah! That's pretty rad. I can always accept extra credit."

"Sounds like you won't need the points with how smart you are, but I have to take what I can get to move out of this hell hole. Teachers don't always try too hard with these basic classes. I think it's a battle between how much effort they should make as our teachers and how much of a return on their effort they'll see. I shouldn't even be in here." She sighed.

"That's a shame," Alex replied, his mouth cocked and brow furrowed in disappointment. "You deserve the same learning opportunities as anyone. Listen, I'll make you a deal. Just come to class, make sure I don't fail since we're partners, and I'll do what I can to help you. Deal?" he offered, picking up the acetaminophen bottle and popping the thin plastic cap.

Ivy watched him peel back the silver airtight foil barrier. She noticed the perfect opportunity to let go of one of her mom's favorite jokes. Her first joke may have fallen short, but she knew this one would crack him. It had to. "Ooh, careful with that," she laughed, watching his face twist into quizzical confusion. "Well, you have to pick cotton to get to the pills. I'm sure you don't want to go back in time." She laughed and locked eyes with her stoic partner. "Oh, do you get it? Because you're, well, you know, black. And that's, um, cotton, like the slaves. You're picking cotton."

"Oh, I get it," he replied sternly. "Do you really think that's a joke?"

Ivy felt herself tremble and she was overtaken by genuine confusion. "Everyone has always laughed. I, um, thought it was a good joke," she shyly replied.

"Have you ever told that joke to a black person?"

"No. I haven't actually met a black person before. I mean, I've talked to one. Of course, I've met one. Well, this has gotten awkward, hasn't it?"

Alex didn't reply. Ivy could feel his eyes locked on her face, scanning her and reading deep into her mind. She heard him deep sigh, a soft but firm breath released through his nostrils. "Moving on. What's the next step?" he said, his words tinged with ice and unspoken limitations on the level of their future interactions.

CHAPTER FIVE

"**H**ow was your first day of school?" Ivy's mom greeted when she walked through the creaky front door, laughing when the thin aluminum frame got stuck in the thickly piled carpet left over from the mid-90s.

"Seriously?" she answered, looking over her mother's disheveled frame. The bags under her eyes were deep indigo and stuck out from her gaunt face like expertly placed throw pillows. Her roots were worse than normal; at least four inches of salt and pepper, wiry strands now stood out from her dull and dry, box dyed chocolate ends. The electric pink nail polish on her rounded nails was chipped, on some nails almost completely off, and her hands looked like they were thirsting for water like a stray puppy lost in the Mojave.

"Now I can't even ask you about school, huh? Your attitude really sucks, young lady," she coughed, a small trail of spittle sticking to the right side of her lips.

"Today wasn't my first day. It's the second, and if you must know, my day was about as horrible as you currently look," she snapped. "What is with you? You look like you haven't showered for days. You smell like it as well."

"I can't help it if life likes to ride me hard and put me to bed wet. You're so ungrateful. I don't know how I got stuck with such an ungrateful, disrespectful child. You know, if your father was still here-"

45

"If Dad was still here? If Dad was still here, you wouldn't be a waitress. If Dad was still here, I wouldn't go hungry half the time because my drunk, selfish mother ate all the food or forgets to buy any. If Dad was still here, we wouldn't be living in this trailer. And, if Dad was still here, you might have some self-decency and self-respect. Don't push your problems on me. I'm sixteen years old, Mom. I should be enjoying life. You know what I shouldn't be doing? I shouldn't be mothering my mother and being reminded what a horrible person I am because I can't successfully mother my mother!"

Tears began streaming down Ivy's face in rapid succession, the cool salty water washing away the thin layer of dust that had unknowingly settled from her stubborn morning walk to school. The words she had just spewed forth were angry and mean, but true. They were her innermost thoughts; thoughts she divulged to no one and kept locked tightly in her mind, safe from causing anyone any harm. Today, however, they were unleashed.

Ivy watched the shock settle over her mother's face. She watched as her eyes flashed angrily and her lips scowled, allowing her smoker's line to sink to a new depth never before seen on her aging face. The anger turned to confusion when her brain continued to cycle through the words. Finally, small crystal droplets began raining down from her dull eyes, catching on her sharp cheekbones until enough collected to spill over and drip onto her worn-out frame. She sobbed a deep, heart-wrenching, genuine sob, the kind Ivy hadn't heard since her father's funeral.

"Today's his birthday, you know," her mother whimpered. "If he were here today, we wouldn't be eating peanut butter sandwiches on discount stale bread that I stole from the donate tray at work. We'd probably be at some nice restaurant, like the Italian Terrace, or Pepper's. You're right, my daughter. I have failed you. You're right."

Ivy stood, frozen. She was used to fighting with her

mother, exchanging hurtful short phrases, bickering and placing blame. She was used to convincing herself that everything wrong in the world was her fault. For the last twelve years, she heard how life would be easier without her, how taxing she was, how much of a physical drain she was, how much money it took to raise her, how much her mother couldn't do because she now had a child. She looked at the broken woman in front of her. For the first time, she realized most of their problems stemmed from her mother's expression of pain. Ivy realized her mother didn't hate her, but saw the only piece of her husband she had left – a piece she wouldn't be able to hold on to forever and would one day, just like her husband, have to let go.

"Today is the eleventh," she whispered, wondering how, for the first time in her life, she had forgotten. Sure, she was fake mad at Magnus, but she had never forgotten her father's birthday before. Terror filled her mind, and she wondered if she was starting to forget. Was this was how it started? When those the dead left behind start missing birthdays, death days, or began to replace their memory with live bodies at holidays? "Don't go anywhere, Mom. Okay? I'll be right back."

"Where are you going?" she sobbed, snot bubbling out of her left nostril, which was swiftly wiped with the back of her left hand. "I don't want to be left alone right now, Baby. You're all that I have."

"I know, Mom. You're all that I have, too. I promise you, I'll be back in half an hour max. Just stay here. Take a nap or something and wait for me, please."

Ivy dropped her treasured black leather backpack to the floor, hearing the heavy textbooks thud against the hollow trailer floor. She patted her pocket, feeling the $10 she had found on the floor of the bus and secretly covered with her right shoe until she could skillfully scoop the crinkled bill up and cram its folds into her pocket. She turned around and looked at the woman's body her mom once occupied and vowed that from this day forward, she would help her mother regain herself and become whole again.

"I'm home," Ivy called, stepping back over the threshold. The living room was empty, and the creak of the thin door echoed throughout the sparsely decorated area. "Mom? Are you home?" she huffed. Anger began to rise from the pit of her stomach. She told her mother not to go anywhere, but like a child, she once again did only what she wanted. The empty room squashed all hope Ivy was beginning to develop for recreating any semblance of a normal life and mother-daughter relationship.

"I'm in here." Her mother's voice softly floated from the kitchen. She was still crying. Ivy had never known her mother to cry; if even a hint of a tear began to form in her dead eyes, the liquid was willfully and expertly commanded away before a trace of weakness could be seen. She had seen hints of emotion, but hadn't seen the raw unleashing of sadness witnessed today since her father's casket was lowered into the ground and the last rose was thrown on top.

Ivy tip-toed towards the kitchen, unsure of what she would find on the other side, hoping her mother was unhurt, alive, and most of all, sober. The thought of her mother somehow buying liquor, or beer, when she didn't even have the desire to buy a loaf of bread to feed them, made her stomach turn. Breaching the corner and peeking into the dimly lit kitchen, Ivy caught her breath. Her mom was not laying on the floor, or bleeding, or surrounded by empty bottles.

"Hey, um, Honey? Can I call you Honey? I don't know what to even call you anymore," she sobbed.

"Ivy," she quickly snapped before roping her defenses back in. "Or Honey. Honey is fine. Anything is fine as long as you actually talk to me." She was whispering, her body quaking with confusion. The want to move forward was strong, but the way how was completely unknown. "What in the world are you doing?"

The yellow speckled countertop was covered in bowls, measuring cups, spoons, any and every baking pan they owned, spatulas, an egg carton, spilled milk, and a half melted stick of butter. A powdery substance was lightly scattered over the counter and in small piles on the floor, toe prints firmly planted around, showing the exact dance of confusion her mother had been doing.

"Well, I'm trying to bake a cake. I had a little bit left over this week. Instead of buying cigarettes, I've been rationing my pack – I want to quit anyway, you know it's not good for you – I picked up some cake mix. You know, so we could celebrate Dad and let him know we haven't forgotten him today. But it's just not working. The bag with all the white stuff exploded, and I'm not sure how much of it I actually need to make a cake. I think my eggs might be bad, they smell kind of funny. I don't remember when exactly I bought them. And the milk is definitely bad, but I think it will just cook like buttermilk and maybe taste okay. I don't know. What do you think? Do you think we'll be okay after everything cooks?"

Her mother continued to frantically ramble while whipping the foul-smelling concoction in a cracked porcelain bowl. Ivy could see tears still dripping down her cheeks, falling into the cake and mixing in with the white batter littered with colorful dots.

"Where in the world did you find eggs and milk?" Ivy asked, knowing their kitchen had been empty.

"Next door. Daryl's. I ran over this morning. I wanted to have the cake ready when you got home, but I was too exhausted. You know Daryl reminds me so much of your dad. Same hair. Same eyes," She sighed, her hands furiously swirling batter with a wooden spoon.

"That's Funfetti," Ivy said. "You got Funfetti."

"Of course. It was your dad's favorite. He said eating the sprinkles was like eating –"

"Little beads of happiness that would soak up any sadness," they said together.

"Hey, Mom," Ivy said, laying her hand on her mother's to slow down her furious whipping. "I think we need to toss this out and start over. It smells really, really, really bad." She laughed, grabbing the bowl and walking over to the sink.

"How can we start over? I only had enough for one box. I just wanted to celebrate him, and I can't even buy a box cake mix right," she sobbed, shoulders heaving and breath shallow as the emotions overtook her body.

"It's okay, Mom. I just went and bought a box, actually. And some fresh eggs, milk, and butter. Let's wash this out, and start over. It's okay. Let's start over."

"Can we start everything over? The cake. This life. Our relationship?" she trembled, kneeling down on the floor with a wet tattered tea towel to begin picking up the small piles of powder that had exploded in the kitchen. "Oh, dear. Would you look at that? I didn't know the floor should be that color," she gasped, watching the water pick up not only the fine powder but also a thin layer of grime that had settled over the ivory flooring in the absence of years of mopping. "I always thought if we didn't wear our shoes, there wouldn't be dirt... Oh, I'm so disgusted. Do we have a bucket? Ivy, Honey, do you know if we even have cleaner?"

Ivy stood at the sink, cleaning the bowl, stunned. She had used a rag in the bathroom before and kept the toilets clean, but she had never cleaned in the kitchen. The kitchen was a room of anger, frustration, and what she had to live without. The kitchen was a room that was supposed to bring her joy and happiness, family bonding and memories of home cooked meals, but always resulted in hunger, headaches, and hatred. If she didn't clean the bathroom or the living room, she knew no one would, and their house would quickly devolve into a soiled pit, but she never realized how she completely ignored the kitchen. Guilt began to sink into her stomach. Today, they would be cleaning the kitchen together, washing away the dirt of their past, while starting a new chapter with little bites of sunshine in memory of someone they both loved dearly.

"Yeah, Mom, we do. It's in the hallway closet, on the bottom shelf. Let me get this new box mixed, and when it's in the oven, we'll start cleaning together. By the time it's cooled, and we can put the icing on, we'll have this place smelling fresh and looking brand new."

"Just like us," her mother whispered.

"Yes, Mom, just like us."

Together, they rubbed, wiped and scrubbed the thin layer of dirt from the floor and cabinets, pausing only to pull the cake from the oven and let it rest, and then once again to slather the thick white icing over the rounded confection. The duo wasted no time and would return immediately to the task of cleaning up the years of neglect that sat between them, mainly working in silence with only a few breaks for small talk.

After the last swipe was completed, the bucket drained, hands washed, and meager supplies tucked back into the hallway closet only slightly larger than her locker, the women admired their work. Just inhaling the pine-scented cleaner lifted their spirits. When their eyes settled on their prize, the thickly frosted uneven cake resting on a plate that was slightly too small, their stomachs growled in unison, and they rushed to grab forks. Not a second was wasted before the bent metal aluminum tines were tearing apart the rainbow dotted spongy flesh.

"I think Dad would be proud of us today," Ivy said, interrupting the feverish eating and moans of pleasure trickling through the kitchen. "Do you believe in heaven? If it does exist ... do you think Dad made it?" Never one to be religious, and always one to be over critical of any restrictive ideology, the thought of her father's soul resting somewhere in comfort occasionally crept into her mind. The thoughts arose every time the number eleven spontaneously popped up during a difficult time, or when she smelled his musk on the wind, or when she had a rare change of luck, like being awarded extra credit just for doing the obvious.

"You know how I feel about all that mumbo jumbo," her mother replied. "But, it's possible. I sometimes wonder if I rebel against the idea because my mother tried too hard to beat into my head the concept of some old man in the clouds judging my every move. Sometimes, it's just scary to think about because you realize that to get there, this ... this right here has to end."

Ivy heard her mom's voice quiver, and she immediately understood what she was really saying. "Is that why you've given up, Mom? Dad's death was hard on me, too Every single day, I wish he called out sick that day."

"I didn't mean to disappear," her mother whispered. "And I didn't mean to blame you or be a horrible mother. I didn't mean to completely give up. And I'm not making any promises, or that I'll be perfect from here on out, or that we won't fight, or that we're always going to have the food we want, but I can promise you that I will try harder. I will make a conscious effort to be your mother again."

"You've said that before. I hope you mean it this time or won't get mad when I remind you that you're not trying very hard."

"I'll do my best."

"Then I will do my best to support you. And I promise that we will eat cake every birthday from here on out. Yours, mine, his," Ivy said proudly. "Now, we have one more thing to do. Well, two, actually." She saw her mother's expression change to a mixture of curiosity and fear, nervously looking around the room for even the subtlest hint of what was to come. "Let's go to the bathroom, we're going to fix that nasty hair and get that nail polish off your fingers."

The dye set in quite nicely, even though Ivy's mom had coarse, aged, and damaged hair. Ivy ran her fingers through each strand, trying her best to get an even coat, and also, to stretch the one box of dye she was able to afford. Unbeknownst to her mother, the sweet-smelling color wasn't just a mousey brown, but subtle chocolate with red undertones. The change wouldn't be so much that it was shocking, but hopefully, just enough to usher in some new energy and self-love.

"Tell me about school. How's it going?" her mother asked, coughing from the fumes that sprinted into her mouth and danced over her tongue.

Well, it's okay. They moved my locker, and it's now in the same bay as the Super Six. I'll probably just carry all of my books every day to avoid making contact with the enemy. Magnus and I have lunch together, so that's good, but I ruined one of his last rich boy shirts yesterday by throwing a piece of dressing soaked lettuce on him as a joke.." Ivy sighed.

"I'm glad you and Magnus get some time together, though. Is he still taking the advanced classes?"

"Of course," she scowled, trying to hide her frustration over spending another year in the lowest level courses when she was hungry to learn and be better. "So, the school forced us to go to a career fair today. They brought in all of these rich and famous graduates and made us sit and listen to how great they are, how much money they make, and then did these stupid question sessions to try and get students to admit they wanted to be them. It was the most self-serving display, Mom," she continued, still scowling.

"Oh, I hated those. All of those uppity pretty people who have had everything handed to them on silver. Put them in the diner for one day, and I bet they'll finally get a wrinkle or a grey hair. They're so out of touch with what life is like for the rest of us."

"I know," Ivy exclaimed, furiously rubbing the dye through the side strands. "They act like all you have to do is go to college. They forget about paying for college, getting letters of recommendation for college, or even being able to take classes that a college will look at as admission quality! They stand up there in their expensive outfits, practically drooling money, to try and convince me to waste my days dreaming about something the world would never let me be? So ridiculous. And get this. Leslie Strafford's doctor dad tried to shame this new kid, but the kid's mother actually won an award the previous year Mr. Strafford had been nominated for. He embarrassed the doctor so bad. I wish you could have seen it because it was classic," she laughed.

"I bet it was. Wealthy privilege embarrassing the wealthy privilege. What a vicious cycle those people lead. I bet that kid is the hottest topic in your class right now because his ego runs his mouth."

"Well, he is the talk of the class....but not really because of that. Well, maybe slightly because of that. But...he's black. The kid, I mean. Can you believe that? I wonder why his parents brought him here instead of downtown or somewhere with people he could actually be friends with. I mean, there's no other black people at our school. Who is he going to hang out with on the weekends?"

"And you said his mom is a big shot doctor? Do you think he was telling the truth about that or just trying to fit in?"

"I think he was telling the truth. The doctor recognized his mom's name and got super awkward. Oh, and guess what? He's my chemistry partner! He's supposedly really good at chemistry, but our administration wouldn't take his credits or whatever. They made him start back at the beginning."

"Well, you can't blame the administration for that,"

Ivy's mom said. "I mean, I wouldn't trust inner city credits, either. All he has to do is join the basketball team or cry, and I'm sure the school will give in to his every demand. You be careful. Don't let him ruin your grade this semester, and if he does, you let me know. We'll get this settled. Do you want me to call the administration tomorrow and try to get you changed?" she asked with genuine concern.

Ivy continued to massage the final squirts of dye through any thinly covered strands, urging her mother to sit still and stop fidgeting. "You know, he's actually really smart. I think he'll be good for me. Well, if he talks to me. He's a little mad at something I said."

Ivy began to explain the madness of the first chemistry class, the official selection of partners, and the basis of the experiment. Excitedly, she relayed how to properly conduct scientific research, monitor the control, keep the components pure and untainted, and how she almost ruined the experiment by sticking her finger into the cola.

"So then, we had to open the acetaminophen so we could get on with the experiment. I cracked the joke about picking cotton when he popped the seal and told him to be careful. He got so mad at me. Can you believe it?"

"Over a joke? Has he never heard that one before? I tell that one all the time and everyone always laughs," her mom replied.

"I know! That's what I said. I explained that to him, too. He just asked me if I'd ever said that to a black person before and seen them laugh, so I had to tell him that I'd never really met a black person before. But I don't understand why he wouldn't find it funny. I mean, I was basically showing him I'm aware of his American history."

"Are you sure you don't want me to try and get your partner changed? I will call tomorrow if you want me to," her mother urged.

"No, I really need him. He's so smart. I just can't joke with him because he has no sense of humor," Ivy said, giving a deep sigh and popping off her rubber gloves. "Okay, Mom. I'm going to set the timer for fifteen minutes. Don't forget to use the conditioner pack, not that dollar store conditioner. We want all the special oils and expensive things they put in their formula to finish your hair off."

"Sounds good, Honey. I'll just sit right here and read about what celeb is doing what other celeb and complaining about how hard it is to be rich," she joked, holding up a glossy tabloid she swiped from the bin outside of the gas station. "Ivy," she paused, locking eyes with her daughter, "thank you for this. For tonight. I love you."

Ivy smiled, a sincere, genuine smile. She noticed the small twinkle that settled into her mother's eyes and the flush settling into her cheeks as her body digested the copious amount of sugar and carbs from their birthday cake dinner. In one night, small glimpses of the woman that once took her to the park and pushed her on the swings, laid down in the floor to color with her, or lovingly ran a warm bubble bath after school, began to creep back in. She hoped they would stay, because even the small pieces of hope made her start to feel like a whole person again. She had felt broken for such a long time that she no longer recognized the shattered fragments of her soul, only the splinters piercing her heart.

"I love you too, Mom."

CHAPTER SIX

"**C**ome on, kiddos. This isn't that difficult," Mr. Green belted down the aisle of the school bus. "Pick a seat and put your butt in it. The longer you take to sit down, the longer it takes us to get downtown, and the less time you'll have to run like rabid dogs around the museum."

Ivy slid into the second seat, hoping no one else would willingly sit in the front and she'd have the seat to herself for the long ride downtown. Field trips were one of the few times she could have solitude, especially if they went to a museum. Not only did she get out of her ridiculously simple and boring classes for the entire day, but the teachers would also be too worried about the true heathens creating drama to even notice she was alive. They knew it was worthless to try and keep the group together. Instead, they'd give a time frame, a map, some simple bullshit assignment like a scavenger hunt, and set them loose. The worksheets were so easy one should be able to finish them without even setting foot in the museum if they just paid attention back in elementary school.

"Seriously, guys, come on," Mr. Green moaned. "Just take a seat! We're going to be on the bus for thirty minutes, and you'll have all day to socialize. Whatever seat you are next to, butt in the seat, right now, or you're getting off and going to your regularly scheduled class."

Immediately, spare bodies dropped with a squeak

against the army green textured vinyl of the bus seats. Their voices, however, stayed above a safe decibel level, with groups of students forgetting that they either don't have to yell across the aisle, or their conversation isn't important enough to be screamed over eight seats.

The bus driver clicked their key into the ignition, pushing the engine to rev and shake in its metal frame before rolling into a gentle purr. Ivy noticed the blinking red light located just over the slanted mirror placed near the ceiling in a thick heavy grey fiberglass frame, indicating this bus trip would be recorded. Turning the camera on was probably the smartest choice anyone on this bus had made. The cool glass window greeted her forehead, and she closed her eyes. With deep breaths flowing in and out with counted precision, the cacophony of the rowdy heathens located behind her slowly turned into a gentle buzz and then disappeared altogether.

In her mind, she was in a sunny meadow, soaking in the sun's warm golden rays while lying on her stomach and furiously flipping through a book. Gentle peaks erupted around her with snowy caps, slowly melting in the cool-ness of the high altitude, sending their pure runoff to fill the quaint lake to her left. Deer gently grazed on the sweet wildflowers, sharing the treat with a colony of busy bees, working hard to pollinate future flowers. In between beau-tiful words that filled her mind, she filled her stomach with a soft red wine, expensive French cheeses she couldn't pronounce, and the type of crackers that broke perfectly with each bite but didn't cover your torso in crumbs.

While Ivy spent her free daily moments dreaming of wide open spaces without another soul in site, crisp, clean mountain air, and freely frolicking wildlife, most of her classmates dreamed of the beach: spring break in Mexican clubs with margaritas, smoking joints in Jamaica, downing shots of Mamajuana in the Dominican, or any other mind-al-tering experience on any tropical location their parents would send them to for a week alone. They would come back with long braids topped off at the end with cheap plastic beads, clacking like a set of toddler's toy keys for the next week until their scalp began to itch, and their parents became annoyed with the constant reminder they would never know exactly what their children were up to with all of their money. The girls would spend the next week complaining about their tan lines while the boys begged to see them, and almost every year, a seedy video would surface showing one of the least expected girls getting a little too drunk and finally reaching the point in her night where she lost all inhibitions. Last year, as a matter of fact, they saw the middle school principal's daughter and head cheerleader participate in a wet t-shirt contest that turned into a wet body contest and was filmed for Girls Get Drunk.

Rumors were strong after that one. The PTO tried to crucify Principal Harris for his daughter's actions, saying he wasn't fit to lead their children when he gently reminded them that most of their children not only drove down to Miami together but rented a house together, and if they looked closely, could be seen in the background drinking. He was the captain of this proverbial ship, and if an iceberg sent them down, they would all go together. Somehow, despite everyone in town talking about the most famous set of breasts in Greenwood, both face to face and on social media, the local papers managed to completely ignore the scandal. The lack of media coverage created another set of rumors that Principal Harris must have been in the mafia, or they had more money than their standard middle-class brick two-story neighborhood house with a pool and three car garage let on. By the time graduation came around, rumors had swirled that we had a secret mafia cell, Principal Harris was an undercover CIA agent, and that, just maybe, he had an undisclosed stake in the state media sources considering our school district rarely had an objectionable piece made public. The newspapers even claimed to not get notified when the town darling lost her full-ride scholarship to Princeton after they were tagged in the video and found her breasts didn't meet their admission requirements.

Ivy could feel the gentle pull of her cheeks, moving her pencil thin, perpetually straight lips into a crooked smile. Even though she didn't take delight in others' misfortune, she did believe in karma and having to receive the consequences of your actions. She was always being reminded that every decision she made had results, so much so that the phrase was almost a battle cry of sorts.

A heavy thunk and rattle shook her head, dissolving her picture-perfect Alpine meadow and melting reality back into an overcrowded, slightly smelly, extremely bumpy school bus careening down the road. Her hair sunk under the heavy weight of an aluminum ball, firmly planted against the rear of her head. With a quick tug, accompanied by a background of laughter, she pulled the sphere from her head, grimacing as she felt the warm stringy leftovers of some sort of melted cheese.

"Bingo," a voice screamed from the rear, riding the waves of laughter that echoed through the metal tube. "That's how you take out the trash."

Ivy wasn't one to shrink and cower from the constant teasing, even though she thought she did her best to avoid giving any of her peers cause to attack. A deep breath slowly moved down her throat, into her lungs, filling them to capacity while her stomach extended. Constricting her diaphragm, the air slowly pushed out to the count of ten. Breath. Repeat. Breath. Repeat, she silently reminded herself, channeling the one yoga class she participated in after accidentally stumbling into an open studio while looking for a bathroom at the YMCA. The instructor insisted she sit down, even though she wasn't a paying participant because he could see the stress furiously scribbled over her forehead.

"Sit. I will release you," she purred. "Just relax and let me show you how to breathe. On this new journey, you will learn to control your environment and your reaction," she promised.

The lesson had been useful to some degree, such as now when she was pretty sure she could feel her strands turning into a birds nest under some stray grease and left-over half eaten cheese that had found her hair to be a more hospitable home than aluminum foil destined for a trash can. For a moment, she managed to tune out the cacophonous roars that threatened her sanity; for a moment, she found herself back in her peaceful meadow where the only distracting noise came from the happy beaks of chattering birds.

The next heavy thump against her head exploded into a mess of shredded lettuce, cubed tomatoes, and a few soupy beans. Every lesson someone pounded into her head through the years told her to be strong, to not engage, or to acknowledge. At the same time, the devil on her left shoulder told her to let it rip and give these assholes every heavy word a strong female's tongue could lash out. If she did fight back, and trouble ensued, she took solace in knowing the bus camera was recording everything and with a snowball's chance in hell, a minutely small but possible chance, she could defend her case.

"Come on, Alex," she heard the heathens call, chanting, cheering on their new favorite toy.

"If you land this next shot, A, we'll make sure you make the basketball team," another promised.

"Oh, please. We need our own future NBA star," another laughed. "You don't have to make him promises. He knows he's in if he just shows up."

Ivy listened, but she wasn't sure if she heard Alex or not. Ever since their first exchange, their relationship was strained at best. Still, she believed with every ounce of her naïve being that he would not participate in an activity like this; he was a better person with an open heart and an understanding of ethical behavior.

Filling her lungs with the deepest breath possible and planning her initial attack, she popped to her feet and turned with the precision of an Olympic figure skater. At the exact same moment, trash missile number three was placed into orbit and with its previous target no longer in place, continued its forward movement until it landed precisely in the middle of the bus driver's head, exploding into a wondrous array of scrambled eggs, sausage bits, and what could possibly be gravy.

She didn't see who launched the final ball that resulted in the bus being pulled over to the side of the road under threats of turning back around, promises of watching the tape and giving every person involved an entire semester of Saturday detention, but when she locked eyes with Alex, his face crimped up with apologetic guilt.

Perhaps she was wrong about him after all.

"Pick up your worksheets BEFORE you get off the bus. These are due when you step back ON the bus. If you do not complete the required activities while you are running around the museum like feral children on triple espresso shots, you will get one week of detention. For some of you, this may mean we're going to get to know each other really well. If you don't want to become my personal best friend and start singing chorus tunes with me when you could be home playing video games, or whatever you kids do these days, finish the worksheet. Does everyone understand?" Mr. Green called. His face was beet red and already exhausted from the drive. He muttered something under his breath that no one heard, but everyone could understand with basic lip reading and began thumbing out the small package of elementary level worksheets that half the class wouldn't finish.

Ivy grabbed her paper last, ignoring Mr. Green's attempt to offer his condolences for the food he picked out of her hair earlier and bounded down the bus stairs to the parking garage. She stayed just far enough behind her classmates to not be seen, but close enough to see what exhibits they were moving to first. They acted like a pack of lemmings; hanging close to each other like they couldn't function on their own and following the slightest movement from whoever was today's leader.

She watched as they disappeared into the corridor that led to the planetarium. After the last body safely moved from her line of sight, she moved up the wide winding ramp that would take her to the top. Her plan of action was simple: move through the top exhibits while everyone was raising hell on the bottom floor. She knew her pace would be slower since she was actually interested in learning. By all estimates, they would meet on the second floor, but, if she finished the top floor and then took the elevator to the basement level, she would miss them entirely as they tore up to the top.

"Welcome to India," a faux airline stewardess greeted her at the first exhibit, ushering her into a hollowed out airplane that served as the introduction to the exhibit. She followed the museum's plan and buckled herself into an airplane seat to watch a video pretending that all the participants were actually on a plane heading to Asia. Ivy appreciated the museum's efforts to be interactive, not stale and standoffish.

When the fake pilot had cleared the fake passengers for their fake landing on the other side of the world, in a record three minutes and ten seconds, she gleefully popped out of the airplane shell into what looked like a street market scene. She could pick up some colorful saris and try to wrap herself, smell different spices, press buttons to fill the room with the hustle and bustle of a densely populated country with a very diverse range of citizens, or she could keep moving into a mock Indian kitchen where an actor would walk her through how to make Indian flatbreads.

Her visions of India were based on the glossy pages of travel magazines, where people had unlimited budgets, private chauffeurs, rooms with Jacuzzis and butlers, and personal escorts around town. In this exhibit, she felt transported to another place and time entirely. What had previously only been one vision presented through careful editing was turning in to a desire to see these markets, kitchens, and fabric stalls for herself. She found herself feeding a deep, intense yearning that she'd never noticed before. Everything around her filled a deep hole in her soul, almost like this exhibit was made just for her, just for what she didn't know she needed.

Tracing the finely embroidered edges of a deep purple sari, she let her mind wander to the women who would sit, surrounded by spools of gold and copper threads, and create majestic patterns out of virtually nothing. The cool smoothness of the fabric slid through her fingers like a fresh mountain brook, gliding with ease and cascading elegantly. She had never felt something so luxurious in her life. To date, her clothes were polyester blends or cheap cotton. The highest thread count she'd ever experienced was from the 200 count clearance cotton bed sheets she crawled in every night. Daydreams of busy streets flowing with exotic spices and beautiful, colorful women filled her mind until the screaming of a large group of unsupervised heathens interrupted her bliss.

"Oh, shit," she muttered, jerking her head around to see the pack entering the exhibit, skipping over the fake airplane while the actress playing the stewardess looking on in frustration. Her eyes scanned the room for the exit, quickly assessing each aisle, walkway, and the museum's desired pattern of movement. She dodged and ducked, watching in horror as some of the boys flicked the fabrics she had previously obsessed over, scrunched their noses, and fake vomited over the spices they couldn't pronounce and teased the chapatti maker with stupid assumptions over a small circular piece of food.

Breaking free from the exhibit without being noticed carried the same adrenaline and temporary relief of a prisoner who had just shimmied down a sewage pipe into a fresh lake or stream to escape their confining cell. She quickly moved down the wide ramp to the basement, hoping the pack wouldn't move back down after they tore up the top floor. Judging by the frustrated staff and excessive presence of janitors running through each exhibit on the floors she scurried past, the pack had already made their mark in these locations.

She ducked into an exhibit boasting hands-on activities for children, hoping the younger target demographic would guarantee a heathen free zone without the need to apologize for her classmates to any museum worker she passed. Looking around, she knew that would not be the case. Small spades and brushes used to imitate a fossil dig were scattered over the floor, piles of sand were shaped like breasts and fingers had proudly traced male genitalia in other sand pits.

"Absolute morons," she muttered loudly, bending over to pick up the sand toys and put them back in their respective homes. She moved towards the sand boobs, knocking them over, and then dusted over the stray penises until they were no longer visible. Anger seethed inside, starting from the very pit of her stomach, which based on her freshman biology class she knew was actually her intestines, and moved up until her heart tightly constricted, and her vision began to float with little specks of what looked like clear segmented worms. That same biology class had explained what those floaters were, but she could only expect herself to retain so much information at once.

"They're pretty ridiculous, aren't they?" Alex replied, sitting on a bench normally reserved for parents keeping an eye on their children, no doubt chased out of a peaceful day at the museum. His homework package was spread out over his lap, and he furiously doodled around the edges. He paused, looking Ivy up and down. "By the way, I didn't throw any of those trash balls. And, I'm sorry they did that to you."

"Well, I wasn't exactly looking at who did or who did not throw them, nor do I care. After a while, it's just another day where you have to know your place. My place here is pretty easy to understand, so don't feel like you have to justify their actions, or your lack of actions, to me," she snapped, running her feet over the floor, trying to push the small grains of escaped sand back towards to the fossil dig pit.

"Why do you let them treat you like that? You don't have to, you know," he said, genuinely interested in why she had given up on her right to a peaceful high school existence.

"Why do you?" she replied. "You were so mad at me over a stupid cotton joke, but you let them talk about how 'your kind' is needed on the basketball team. I suppose it's okay to be racist and judgmental as long as it's somewhat positive?"

Alex eyed her intensely, contemplating how to respond. "I understand what you're saying, I do. But, those two situations are different, Ivy. Your joke was really ignorant."

"But the guys you're so desperate to fit in with aren't ignorant for pushing you to join a sports team just because you're black? All black people are the next Kobe Bryant, so it's cool, right?" she barked.

"No, it's not. Like I said, I do understand what you're saying, but I don't think you understand what I'm saying –"

"I do understand what you're saying," she interrupted. "You're setting limits for just how racist people can be with you, and who you're willing to take it from. Are you scared of them? Or do you realize that I'm just not a threat, so you can stand up to me and make yourself feel a little bit better?"

"You're really crossing some lines," he replied, his legs nervously bouncing. "I mean, okay. Fine. I suppose I do let them get away with some things. But...well...you know what? I don't know how to explain this to you, and I feel like you don't want to recognize the difference between you cracking jokes about slavery and them assuming I'm good at sports. I don't have the energy for this today. Google it when you get home." Alex took a deep breath, calming his body and giving his paperwork a flip to snap the thin sheets into place.

"Google it when I get home? Google what, Alex?" Ivy huffed.

"I don't know, Ivy. Why not try how to talk to black people as a start? Or maybe, how to not be racist post-2010?"

"That sounds like a great idea there, Alex. I'll tell you what, I'll even print out what I find and give a full report to your buddies, too." Ivy scrunched her face, not even trying to mask her frustration or the tantrum threatening to boil up and spill from her tightly curled lips. "You know what? I don't have time for this, or you, or your drama, or your name calling." She threw her hands up, snapping her papers forward to mock her lab partner's previous actions.

"Kids," Mr. Green sighed, his patience running low, exhaustion floating out of his oversized body with every breath, "we are not doing this again. Sit your asses down in a seat, no talking, no throwing, nothing. Do nothing. We will be obtaining security footage for those of you who left male genitalia in the fossil dig sandpit, curse words in the magnetic letters of the toddler's exhibit, and who the hell knows what else I'm going to get an email about tomorrow." Subtle laughter trickled through the bus accompanied by the soft slapping of high fives and childish congratulations.

"Well," he continued, "it sounds like you're really proud of yourselves. Some of you will have a lot of Saturday school, some others a good few months of detention, but all of you, yes, all of you, will now have two weeks to prepare a full research project for the school science fair. If you do not complete your project, well, you fail, and we'll see each other next year. Possibly even the year after that the way some of you are going."

The collective groans and loudly placed complaints dripping with profanity brought a smile to Ivy's face. Some people would always need to be shown they weren't as tough as they thought, as important as they felt, or as indestructible as they tried to portray. There would always be people who thought they were above rules, more significant than the status quo, or trying to drown their insecurities by spreading their negativity like a black pool of death to any who were unfortunate enough to get too close. In her mind, she watched the news stories roll out; newscasters would wrinkle their noses and sigh in disgust next to small inset video showing her classmates running amok. They would shame their parents, shame the school, and shame the heathens. But, she knew the next frame would also be praising the same kids for being star athletes, scoring the winning touch down, the tie-breaking goal, the final home run, or some other redeeming event to re-humanize and de-villify the chosen ones.

"Now, about your science fair projects," Mr. Green chuckled. "You'll need to get with your lab partners and decide on a theme this week. Your initial hypothesis and research plan must be turned in by Friday. That means you have three days to decide on your plan of action, type it up, and put it in my hands. Those of you who fail to do so will fail the project, and even though you're not rocket scientists, that means you will also fail the course. And, you will not be doing this during class. Our regularly scheduled projects and experiments will continue per the syllabus. If you want to run around and act like decision-making adults, it's time you managed your schedule and future like adults."

"Wait, Mr. Green," Alex called from the back. "Did you say we have to work with our lab partners? Is that negotiable?"

Ivy turned around furiously, the realization settling into her mind at the same time Alex spoke up. "Mr. Green," she gushed, "are you sure we can't pick our own partners this time?"

"I'll take Alex," Adam Salvo quickly replied. "Anyone would take Alex, moron. It's a guaranteed A." He locked eyes with Ivy, his face freshly washed with judgment and victory, causing Ivy to seethe with disgust.

She knew she should be jumping with joy; she was fortunate enough to be partnered with the smartest kid in the class, if not one of the most intelligent kids in the school. Anyone on this bus would be lucky to be in her shoes, but here she sat, gladly begging for the opportunity to be stolen, even if it meant she would have to carry the work of her science fair project completely on her own shoulders. Doing all of the work couldn't possibly be any worse than being stuck working with some hypocritical, self-assured, two-faced wanna-be in disguise, who had the audacity of calling her a racist. She may be a lot of things: poor, trailer trash, boring, and average, but deep down, she knew she was not a racist, and certainly not more than anyone else that sat on that bus with her.

"Zip it, kiddos. The rules have been very clearly stated. This is non-negotiable, which in case you didn't know, means we are not discussing or changing any rules, partners, deadlines, or expectations. Now, sit down, shut up, and keep the bus clean."

Ivy stared at Alex. She knew he could feel her eyes boring deep cavernous trenches into the side of his face. And, she knew he was staring out the window, purposely evading her intense gaze, because his deep brown eyes occasionally flickered towards her and then quickly back towards the moving road. When he finally gave in and turned to lock eyes with Ivy, she felt the same emotions being sent back with The air was slowly sucked out of her lungs and she broke, turning back around in her seat. Her hands gripped the leathery back in front of her for stabilization as the bus started to spin in circles around her still body.

CHAPTER SEVEN

*I*vy sat on the rough concrete steps leading to her front door, running her fingers over the rusted but delicate floral filigree that composed the thin iron banister, supposedly in place to keep people from toppling over the edge. When she looked closely, she fell in love with the twists and turns of the curls, the delicate spirals of the long primary spires, and the intricacies of the flower petals. Each delicate leaf looked like they were alive and blowing in an imaginary breeze instead of cast in metal only to be neglected in some poorly kept front yard. She always felt that beautiful pieces like this should be reserved for castles or mansions, some-where they would be carefully wiped down, probably oiled, and painted bi-yearly when the edges started to become weathered. If something this beautiful was accessible for a family of such small means, she could only dream of what greeted visitors at some of the world's grandest estates.

The honking of an old horn pulled her from her visions of grandeur. The grainy huzzah started as a tweet and slowly simmered down to the snore of a slumbering giant. The soft rattle of a loose exhaust almost sounded like the softly clopping horses trotting down the cobblestone drive of her imaginary castle. Unfortunately, this wasn't a grand Clydesdale with thick cuffs of fur floating in the breeze with each elegant step at her driveway. This was a horse of a different color, - three different colors to be exact. Magnus recently purchased a 1985 Mustang from the local junk-yard with a small sliver of his accessible savings. A very small sliver - $460 to be precise.

"Come on, Sleeping Beauty. I don't have all day to sit here and wait for you to wake up. Let's go," he called, his voiced muffled by the window that would only roll down halfway due to a stuck gear.

"Do we have to? I really don't want to do this," she replied.

"Do you want to be a sophomore in beginner's Chemistry your entire life? Didn't think so. Get your butt in this car."

Her brown leather sandals stuck to the pavement with each step as if the grey tiles were quicksand in some remote Amazonian jungle. The will to keep moving forward was a valiant effort, but she preferred enticing rewards at the end of challenges. This struggle was only moving her baby step by baby step closer to her lab enemy's house to finish their necessary research.

"I can't believe you got a car," she laughed, tugging on the flaking silver handle. The door finally creaked and gave way with a pop. She sunk into the patchy velour racing seat and squealed with a mixture of pain and shock.

"Oh, yeah. The springs in that seat are a little, well, worn. You have to sit down softly and try not to move. I'm afraid one of them will give up soon and puncture someone right up the rectum," he laughed.

Ivy returned his laugh, the strong visual image of dying in this car by a stray spring shooting up her backside was too b-horror movie for this morning. "I take my previous statement back. I can't believe you got THIS car."

"Have you ever gone car shopping? I'd be lucky to even get a bicycle for what I paid for this puppy. Trust me, Ivy. Once I get this sweet hunk of steel and aluminum fixed up, she's going to be a real classic. People will be falling over their own feet to buy her from me."

She? Isn't that an insult to women?"

"I think it's a testament to this baby's strength. Don't be so judgmental. Lots of good men, women, boys, and girls, start as fixer-uppers. Lots of people start off as a collection of mismatched, broken pieces that they fix one by one. It's not the quickness of the journey but the honesty of the progress."

"You're so meta, Mag," she laughed.

"Or maybe we're just as broken as this car, but only one of us is interested in working on getting our pieces back together."

The mismatched car shook, struggling to get down the soft hills lined with perfectly manicured trees, expensively plotted landscaping, and careful attention to curbside appeal. The yards of the larger houses, if you could call them houses when they looked like hotels or museums, approached the street with their alternating green stripes topped off with boring metal black bars, wide enough to showcase the beautiful mansions spreading out against the horizon but close enough together to keep curious bodies from slipping through. Although all the way out here, in the safety and comfort that money buys, she doubted the bars kept strangers out as much as loved ones in.

Ivy did her best to not gawk or make any snide comments. The whole lettuce on the shirt incident was still fresh in her mind. She wasn't entirely sure if there was an underlying current of tension still floating between them, or if that was her guilt lingering. Even though she wasn't entirely sure where he previously lived, she was almost positive his former life existed in the sprawling estates and stucco mansions that surrounded them now. The tense way his hands held the wheel and his body sat rigidly in his seat out of stress, not because he was trying to avoid a spare spring popping out, told her she was right.

"What's the lab partner from hell's address?" he asked; his voice monotone with a slight hint of a quiver. Ivy dug around for the small yellow square of paper that had the address scribbled in green ink. "You really need a phone. They have this amazing thing called text messaging and GPS maps. These are especially handy when someone else is driving you to your final destination. You never told me why you hate this kid, either."

"Ah! Found it. 2243 Timber Rail Circle. Should be just around the corner according to these directions."

"Yeah, it's just up here," Magnus replied. "I know where it is."

"Good. What a relief. You've been there before, then?" she asked, shoving papers back into her bag and pulling the zipper tightly back in to place.

"You could say that," he stammered. "It's, um, that's my old house."

The Mustang turned in between brick columns breaking up one of the iron fences, squeaking down the elegantly paved cobblestone driveway and over a small bridge that curved through a manicured grove of birch trees. Vines wound around the tree trunks, popping brilliant shades of emerald and chartreuse against the peeling white bark. Trails of marigolds, pansies, and ornamental cabbages wound together into elegant designs.

"Wow," Ivy whispered, carefully choosing her next words in an honest effort to keep the pain from spreading further over Magnus' face. "If I had known, I wouldn't have asked you to drive me, Mag. This is...beautiful. You must have had a beautiful childhood."

"Yeah," he softly replied. "We were lucky. Running through here as a child was, well, magical. It was like playing in your own private fairy tale. I haven't even driven by here since my grandmother sold the place. I'm really happy to see they've kept the magic going."

Ivy heard him choke and her heart sank. "Do you want me to see if you can come inside?"

"No," he replied firmly. "No. I don't want to go any farther."

Reaching over the crooked center console, truly understanding the pain and challenges Magnus had faced with his quickly changing lifestyle, she was taken back to the day her dad died. She couldn't help but think about her mother's downward spiral that she blissfully ignored and used to create a divide, and how heartlessly she joked instead of leaning on someone who actually understood the same pain in a lifetime chance of healing.

"Do you want me to find another ride home? I don't mind, Mag."

"No. I told you I'd drive you. You'll be done at eight, though, right? I just want to make sure I'm here on time, not a second too early." His voice trembled harder as the grove of trees slowly opened, revealing a breathtakingly majestic mansion. Portions of stucco that climbed up what may have been two, possibly three stories offset the off-white brick foundation. A soft green tin roof, the kind that comes with a pre-decorated patina but continues to age with grace, capped the house. Matching shutters framed the paned windows she was sure reached from floor to ceiling. "Do you mind if I drop and run?"

"I wish I could understand, Mag, but I don't. And for that, I'm really sorry."

"Don't be silly, you understand more than you know. You've lost dreams, too. Now, go. Finish your research and maybe tonight, after I pick you, we can go eat our feelings at Steak N' Shake."

"That sounds wonderful. I swear you can read my mind."

The doorbell's hollow chimes filled the foyer with a melodious song; tinkering filled the space and spilled out through the ornate glass door to where Ivy was standing on the porch. The sound was soothing, sweet, and the very definition of welcoming; a complete 180 from their generic 'someone's here' announcement. If Alex's doorbell were an opera singer, Ivy's doorbell would be a three pack a day smoker with a case of chronic bronchitis.

She watched him approaching the door; his shoulders were hunched, head down, and he refused to make eye contact. There were still very tall walls in place. Promising to not put any more bricks in the mysterious wall she was quickly building, she knew the only way to proceed was to open up first and try her best to be friendly.

"Hey there, partner. Ready to study?" she bubbled.

"You found it," he sighed, rolling his eyes and reluctantly pulling the door open just enough to let her slip in.

"Yeah, we found it. Do you know my friend Magnus?"

"No. Should I?"

"No," she cringed, trying to fight back the annoyance rising in her throat.

"No, you shouldn't. But I guess this was his house. Before his parents died. He technically inherited it, but his grandma sold it while he was at summer camp. He, um, lives by me now."

She watched curiosity push through his tough-guy defenses and a softness settle over his shoulders

"That's intense. If it helps, he's welcome to come by any time, if it's not too weird."

"I don't think he's ready for that, yet, but thank you. So, the experiment. What do we need to do for this?"

Alex walked Ivy to the back yard, crossing through a living room easily four times larger than her trailer with pristine white furniture. If the elegant camel back couch had been in her house, the thick down filled cushions would be in grave danger of never being white again. It's not that they were messy, things just happened to collect copious amounts of dust and small splatters of who knows what from who knows where at no particular time. Even if she or her mother didn't sit on the couch for a week, a new tiny spot would spring up, making firm eye contact with Ivy every time she passed by.

The stark but inviting living room moved into a kitchen with more counter space than she thought one family could possibly ever use. The duo walked towards the back of the house where clear stained-glass floral patterns made up the French doors, opening onto a three-tiered deck, masterfully winding its way down a series of ornate staircases to a waterfall bordered pool. Just beyond the edge of the pool was a full-size basketball court with poles off to the sides, allowing a quick conversion to a tennis court.

"I thought you meant you had a driveway hoop with some spray-painted lines or something," Ivy stammered. "That's a full size...what do you call them? Arena? Diamond?"

Alex laughed, but not in a way that demeaned her or made her feel any more awkward than she already was – if that was even possible. "It's a court. Basketball and tennis, actually. Both are played on a court. I can get a can of spray paint and make some marks if that makes you feel better."

Ivy appreciated the attempt to lighten the tension that hung between the two of them. A tiny glimmer of hope sparkled in the air, hinting that perhaps the rift between them could be patched. "No," she giggled in return, "you don't need to deface your property. Do you have chalk, though? I think we should at least mark our spots out so we can keep our experiment controlled."

"Oooh, look at Madame Scientist coming to join the party! I don't have chalk, because I'm not eight, but I did pull out some duct tape. I went ahead and measured the spots out just to save some time."

"Isn't that just great? Less time to prepare means more time to make a fool out of myself when you realize I have no idea how to shoot a basketball. I don't know how I let you talk me into doing our project around statistics of shooting, or whatever we're doing."

"If I remember correctly," Alex began with an 'I told

you so' look on his face, "I didn't talk you into the project at all. That king-sized attitude of yours suggested we do this when you still felt like you had something to prove to the world."

Ivy cringed. He wasn't exactly wrong. The rules for the science fair were clearly laid out, and they both knew to come to an agreement on a topic wasn't going to be easy. In the midst of an argument over what would be a winner, a loser, too easy, too hard, too impractical, or too egotistical, she had to pop off and suggest they do something basketball centered so Alex could show off like the royalty he thought he was. Exasperated, he agreed, and she knew he only wanted to shut her up.

One of these days, she may learn to let her down her guard, deflate her pride, or accept responsibility for her problems. One day, but most likely, not today.

"You won't laugh too hard? Promise?" she laughed, knowing full well Alex would be in hysterics shortly and hoped his howling wouldn't delay their progress.

The sun began its slow and theatrical dive towards the horizon, trading soft, vibrant blues for electric pinks and highlighter yellows. The crisp late fall air was exchanged for the dark chill of winter that wraps your body and teases the bone-chilling cold on the way. A thick broth wafted on the subtle breezes, dropping hints of tomato, onion, and butcher quality meats on the hungry teenage tongues.

"That smells so good. Your mom must be a great cook," Ivy said, her stomach growling in agreement.

"My mom doesn't cook. Well, rarely. She's usually too exhausted, so we have a cook that comes during the week. Smells like beef stew," he replied, his nose pointed towards the house like a wolf hunting prey.

"You have a cook? Why not just eat those little freezer meals if she doesn't want to cook?"

"Ew, gross," he gagged. "Do you even know what's in those? They're barely able to qualify as food."

Ivy felt herself shrink. There were many nights she would have gladly taken a microwaveable freezer meal. Up until this moment, she had always seen them as a luxury, like the one skillet beef and noodle meals that go from powder to creamy pot of comfort in twenty minutes or less. She did her best to hide her shame, but she was finding it harder and harder to understand her place. She couldn't say the right things that didn't upset him, and what was every day normal for her was located around six feet under the lowest rung on his ladder. Her mind was furiously trying to decipher just how delicious this soup would be if her lab partner considered Beef-A-Bundle to be extremely low-quality food.

She glanced at her watch, thankful the hands were creeping closer to 8 p.m. If she could escape, she would have no worries. She would be able to burrito herself into her flannel bed cover, open the pages of a good book, and throw down some generic dollar store mac and cheese. For her, that was the perfect night. And while she was steeped in thoughts of how different they were, she vowed that even if she somehow became a millionaire one day, she would always appreciate and indulge in the simple pleasures of the life she had been granted from the beginning.

"Hey, listen. I have to meet Magnus at the end of the driveway at eight. I'm going to go ahead and start walking that way. I think we have all of the shots, angles, measurements and trials completed. Do you think we need another round for the experiment, or this is okay?"

"I think we're good. Looks good to me. So I will type up the report if you do the board. I'll send you any specific details that we may want to include by tomorrow afternoon, and if you have any questions or need any help, I'm just a phone call away."

Ivy nodded in agreement. Alex would have high expectations for their final project board. Winning, or even placing, in the science fair would help him move up to the class he should be in, or at least make up for the misplacement on his college application. She knew he was itching to move classes at the end of the semester. This meant she would either be absorbed into an existing group like a phantom limb, or she'd be on her own. She really hoped she'd be on her own. It was much easier to manage your own responsibilities instead of those who had no interest in your success. Even if she wasn't going to be successful, per se, she didn't have to give up on life and be nothing.

Soft amber beams swept over the court, pulling Alex's attention towards the house. "Mom's home. Might as well come meet her before you run down. It'll be quick," he assured, no doubt taking notice of the anxiety that quickly took root, causing Ivy's body to tightly lock in place.

"What do I say to her? I've never met someone famous before. I've never even met a doctor before except for the school nurse and the occasional fake doctor at the pharmacy quick check."

"Chill," he laughed. "She's not famous, and if you think she is, she'd prefer to not know that. Just treat her like you would any human being."

Alex stood up and collected the papers, tapping them gently against the court's asphalt before handing them to Ivy. If she didn't know better, she'd say he may finally be forgiving her for whatever grudge he was holding over a stupid joke.

They quickly wound their way up the steps that felt so much easier to tackle on the way down. Ivy marveled at how easily Alex danced his way to the top. Even though she wasn't unhealthy, she certainly wasn't maintaining any semblance of cardiovascular health. Making a mental note to look at Pinterest when she got home, she decided this would be a good year to start some sort of fitness plan.

"Hey Ma," Alex greeted, holding the back door open to

show Ivy inside. "And Dad. Good to see you home. How was China?"

"Good to see you, Son. Business as usual. Lonely without my best buddy around," he replied, giving his newspaper a flick to tighten up the pages. He sipped from a cup of steaming coffee in his free hand before giving Alex a perfect, toothy white smile. "Want to give your old man a big 'Welcome Home' hug?"

Alex groaned and then laughed. "No, Dad. I missed you, too, but no. This is Ivy, my lab partner," he firmly stated, clearing his throat. "She's on her way out, though."

"Oh, forgive me," his mother said, setting down her tablet and walking over to say hello. Ivy watched her glide over the herringbone wood floor. Not only was she visually elegant, every inch of her body from her meticulous braids, to her glistening smooth skin without a hint of an under eye wrinkle, to her perfectly manicured hands and her never-ending legs, moved with grace, like water sliding over the top of glass. "It's been such a long day at work. We're not used to Alex having friends over. I'm Leticia, this is my husband, Demetrius." She extended a palm, and Ivy wasn't even remotely surprised to notice her hands were as smooth as a newborn's.

"Leticia and Demetrius?" Ivy whispered. A slight chuckle escaped, but not so far that it made its way past everyone's ears.

"Are we making things awkward? I'm so sorry if we're making you nervous," Leticia replied.

"It's just...well, not to be rude, and honestly I don't think this is rude, but you never know with that one over there," she laughed, pointing at their son, not picking up on any of the room's quickly tightened muscles, tense shoulders, or narrowed eyes that were now facing her. "Is Alex short for something? Like Jamiroquai?" she smirked, surrounding the final name with exaggerated air quotes.

"I'm sorry, I don't understand," Leticia said, cocking her head.

Ivy laughed. "You know what I mean. You two have typical black names, but your son is Alex. I know Jamiroquai won't look as good on a resume, but why pick such a... neutral name?"

"For one, Jamiroquai is a band," Demetrius flatly replied. "Leticia, do you want to take this one? I don't have the energy."

Leticia cut in. Her tone was calm but firm. "I'm sorry, did you just say typical black names?" She paused, raking her eyes over Ivy's flesh. Ivy could feel every inch of her body burn under the scrutiny. "Alex, did you say this was your lab partner? The same one that cracked jokes about picking cotton?"

"Yes," Alex sighed.

"She did what?" his father gasped, setting his coffee cup down with a clink so strong Ivy wondered how the bottom didn't bust out against the marble countertop of the breakfast bar.

"No, no," Ivy cut in, waving her hands, eyes as wide as a full moon reflected over a rippling lake at midnight. "I mean, yes, I did say a joke, but...I have no idea what's going on right now or why you are looking at me like this. I just thought, I mean, I guess since he has a white name that you would, too. But maybe your black names, made life hard for you, so you wanted to make Alex's life easier –"

"Ivy," Alex fiercely cut in.

The bottom rims of her eyes started to bulge and fight to contain the rapidly forming queue of water threatening to spill forth. The back of her throat clenched, instantly sucking every inch of moisture from her mouth as it shut off her head from the rest of her body. Without another word, she turned on her heels and scampered to the front door, throwing it open and sprinting down the curved side-walk path. She didn't slow down but kept running until she reached the end of the driveway where she collapsed.

Her watch read 7:54.

These would be the longest six minutes of her life.

CHAPTER EIGHT

"Are you going to tell me what happened on Friday?" Magnus asked, rapidly drumming his fingers on his classic Levi's. "Did he hurt you? You said he didn't, but are you lying to me?" His breathing was rapid and shallow. Ivy noticed bags under his eyes and lines of worry sprouting over his face.

"No," she whispered.

"Well, you haven't returned my calls all weekend. You wouldn't answer your door. Or your email. Or your messenger. You can't tell me nothing happened," he exclaimed.

Ivy hushed him, overcome with anxiety. She spent the weekend furiously gluing, painting, coloring, cutting and crafting pieces for the science fair project board to clear her mind. She cleaned, organized, and detailed the house to push away thoughts of returning to school on Monday.

But here it was, Monday. She was going to have to face Alex in class, and she knew things were not going to go well. He wouldn't even respond to her emails about the project.

"I don't know, Magnus. He's so judgmental and makes a big deal out of nothing. He's a total dick, and I'm afraid it's going to ruin our science fair project. He practically kicked me out of his house the other night."

She waited for Magnus to reply, but she could tell he was digesting the little bit of information she had willingly given up. If she let him chew on the words any longer, he'd start coming to conclusions of his own, and that would not be good for her.

"Okay, so the first day, in Chemistry, I cracked a joke when we were starting our lab experiment. He got pissed off at me and would barely talk to me for weeks. Then, on the field trip, we ran into each other in the basement exhibit where they have that fossil dig for the kids. I thought things were going to be better, but he brought the joke back up and called me a racist, but then I told him the other boys were just as racist, then, but he wouldn't listen to me, and –"

"Girl," Magnus cut in. "You're making my head spin. I need you to focus, take a breath, and slow down. Why is he calling you a racist? Is he just pulling the race card?"

"Yes! For no reason at all except that he doesn't have a sense of humor. When we were doing the experiment, he had to open a bottle of acetaminophen so we could dissolve the pills in these different solutions. He popped the seal. I told him to be careful picking the cotton. He got so pissed off at me and just wouldn't let it go," she gasped, slowing herself to take a breath.

"Oh my God," Magnus whispered.

"I know," she exclaimed in reply.

"No, Ivy. That's bad." Magnus paused, scanning her face for any sort of recognition or understanding. "Ivy, you can't do that or say things like that. Is that why you two fought at his house?"

"No. Wait a minute. Whose side are you on Magnus? You're my friend, not his. It was just a stupid joke." She threw her arms across her body, slumping in the seat. Anger seethed and coursed through her veins. "We fought at his house because I met his mom and dad and asked a question they didn't like. He basically kicked me out."

"No," Magnus replied, shocked. "Ivy...are you serious right now? Please tell me this is all a joke and you're fucking with me."

"Magnus," she screamed. "What is there to joke about? I didn't do anything wrong. He's overreacting, and you're taking his side. I mean, you weren't even there on the bus. The boys were saying things about how they need him to join the basketball team, and I'm pretty sure he threw an old breakfast burrito wrapper in my hair, even if he said he didn't do it. I know he did. I can tell. But my point is that he got mad at me for cracking a joke about cotton in a pill bottle but doesn't care that people assume he's good at basketball because he's black."

"They assume he's good at basketball because his dad was in the NBA and now recruits players from Asia, Ivy. Please tell me you at least see what's wrong with joking about picking cotton?"

Her eyes snapped to meet his. She wished she could shoot daggers from her pupils. She would be happy knowing Magnus could feel her brewing hatred at his betrayal. If anyone could take a joke, or understand a joke, it should be Magnus. They always told each other stupid jokes and loved to take spare coins from the couch down to the convenience store for nickel taffy coated in riddles and ridiculous puns.

"You know what, Mag? You're supposed to be my friend, not his. I don't understand why everyone is so in love with that jerk. When you get over your boy crush, come find me. Until then, don't talk to me."

"Ivy," he sighed.

"No, Magnus. As of right now, you and I are not friends." She snapped up her treasured black leather backpack and stepped out of his car, walking into school alone.

If Monday was as emotionally frosty as the first winter's snow, the rest of the week was a blizzard. By the time Friday rolled around, Ivy had ice running through her veins, and Siberia was now located where her heart used to be. She had barely said two words by choice and proudly resumed riding the bus. She didn't mind sitting in the front by the seventh graders, as long as she didn't have to sit by Booger Barry.

Setting up for the science fair project was a breeze. There was no fuss, no messing with the board, not even a single word exchanged between her and Alex. Ivy came in, untied the yarn holding the project board together, and pulled open the tri-fold display. She pulled down on the cardboard hoop she had carefully crafted and placed at the top and then spread out the skirt she had made for under the board, perfectly mimicking the arc on the basketball court where they took their shots. Countless hours had gone into making this board, and she was extremely proud of her work.

Scanning the room, she noticed no one else's board even compared in terms of detail, presentation, or aesthetics. Even the rich kids, with their fancy tricks, glitter, machine cut accents and fancy add-ons made to look expensive couldn't compare to the final project she had put together. She really hoped Alex would be satisfied and maybe, they would even talk things through. Maybe.

"Must be nice to have Alex for a partner." Ivy looked up to see one of the Super Six, Courtney Cummings: gymnast, cheerleader, yearbook, student council, 4.0, expensive clothes, perfect hair, and anything else you could list here that you might want in your life, but someone else gets without any effort. "I wish I could have sat back and let my partner do my entire project to save my ass," she smirked.

"Thanks, Courtney. I actually did the board, though, and I put a lot of effort into doing it. I don't have parents willing to pay a maid to do my homework so I can go sleep with half the town. That's how you aced Calculus, isn't it? Sleeping with Mr. Meyer?"

The rumors had been all over the school for the last year. Everyone knew a sophomore would never be in

Calculus, let alone ace the class. Some people said they saw the grade report before finals and there was already an A in place for her test result. Others said they saw him pounding her from behind on his desk after school one night. Usually, when there was more than one witness, more than one story, and more than one way to get to the conclusion, a thorough experiment had been conducted, and multiple research paths had been laid down.

"I earned that A. Not that you would know what it means to work hard or to try and make something out of yourself. You're so complacent with just being a bitch to everyone and failing at life. Grow up, Ivy," she snapped.

Ivy was shocked; someone knew her name. She spent so much time in the background ignoring everyone, trying her hardest to send out vibes that screamed stay away or I will cut you instead of vibes that screamed she was desperate and would do anything to join their dark side.

"Everything okay here?" Alex questioned, suddenly appearing at the side of the table.

Ivy didn't know where he came from or how long he had even been around. Her breath hitched, her mind whirred over how to respond. Was everything okay? If it wasn't, what could he do – or would he even care?

"Courtney, if you're going to be a monster to people and mock them for not having all of the privileges that you have, please go excuse yourself somewhere else. Don't do it in my space," he said calmly, looking her square in the eyes, practically toe to toe with the monster herself – one of the many monsters that didn't have to hide in the cavernous depths of here. No, here she could roam freely, eating small children and spitting out their bones at will. "I'm sorry, did I not make myself clear? This is a serious event that impacts our grades. This is not the time for some grade school quality feud to unroll and create drama. Please, excuse yourself."

Ivy swelled with happiness, watching Courtney's eyes narrow and her skin gets flushed. She was mad – no, she was livid. She was a sort of angry Ivy hadn't seen in a teenager before. If today were a Disney movie, this would be the place in time where one of the sweet girls of the village turned into the evil villain making promises to end them all.

"Thank you," Ivy laughed, watching Courtney stomp away.

"Oh, that wasn't for you. That was for me. I don't have time for either of you. I have one goal – pass this semester and get out of this class. Now, excuse me," he said, turning towards the gymnasium exit.

Ivy watched him maneuver his way through the crowd until he was out of sight. She stood by their project, shocked and angry. The entire weekend was dedicated to this project, to that board, and putting her heart and soul into trying to impress her lab partner to smooth over whatever mistake she had made that she still didn't understand.

The gymnasium grew around her. The tables seemed to get taller, the projects larger, the voices louder, and the crowd heavier. She realized she was alone, quite possibly the only person in the gymnasium who was alone. She had no friends, no parents, not even a moderator asking her questions. Every breath she inhaled felt like the room was being broken into minute particles and sucked into her lungs. Every exhale only seemed to forcefully expand the room.

She had no choice but to run. Every neuron, every receptor, every brain wave in her body was on fire, moving signals from her pink slimy command center to her feet. Her body obeyed before her conscience grasped the situation. She didn't try to move delicately or avoid confrontation. There was only one goal this time: to exit the room as quickly as possible, even if it meant running over the massive hardwood court like a bull in a china shop.

Storm clouds sat on the horizon bringing the light scent of

redemption on the cool breezes that tousled Ivy's hair. She sat on the tall concrete curb, firmly planted on the yellow paint that indicated this is not the place for someone to stop, and hugged her knees to her chest. This was the place for her to stop, and she would stubbornly stay here until the charcoal clouds dropped their little droplets, finally giving her free reign to let her own escape. She couldn't remember a single year, or even a single day, when she had cried so much in her entire life. She was positive her second year of high school had already brought more tears than even the fading memories of her father. She hoped this would be a thunderstorm so she could stream into the downpour without being heard.

"Ivy," a voice screamed angrily. "What are you doing? Why did you... What is wrong with you?"

She turned to see Alex scrambling out of the glass atrium doors. He moved like a rabid jackrabbit down the concrete steps until they were face to face on the curb for quick pick up and drops, but not for stopping or standing, which they were both currently doing.

"Oh, great," she sighed. "What did I do now? I haven't even talked to you. I couldn't possibly have said something you would get offended by. I haven't run into any of those bitches out here, so you couldn't possibly need to defend any of your precious better than my friends. So tell me, Alex. What am I doing, why did I do what, and what exactly is so wrong with me?" She didn't wait for the thunder to appear and drown her screams. She released her voice freely and loudly, letting the wind carry her frustration as it tightly hugged the red brick corners of the enormous high school.

"Our project! I just, I never thought you would do something like this," he yelled back. "This was my only chance to get out of this class, and because you can't just be happy for someone, or work with someone, or not be a total miserable lump all the time, you had to go and ruin this for me. This isn't a joke to me, Ivy. This is my future. I need to get out of this class for my college applications!"

"Alex, what are you talking about? I left the gym almost exactly after you did. I don't know how long I've been out here. I know it's been a while, and I know I'm going to sit right here until either the rain floods the world and washes me away or until someone remembers they have to give me a ride home."

"Oh my God. You're always so damn dramatic. You're such a liar, Ivy," he said, his voice trembling. "Just tell me why you did it?"

"Did what?" she screamed, releasing her inner banshee.

"Why did you trash our project? I got called up for our interview, which no shock you weren't around for, and our board was in pieces, my report was ripped to shreds, and we've been disqualified. DISQUALIFIED, Ivy," he screamed, the veins in his neck popping out and his eyes threatening to dislodge from their sockets.

"Wait...what? Oh, Alex, I didn't... I've been out here. I need to pass this class, too. I would never do anything to hurt anyone else..." she stammered.

"If you didn't do it, then who did?" he stomped.

"Well, it may not be much, but my money would be on Courtney or her band of short-skirted heathens. That would be the obvious bet, wouldn't it?" she snarled. Taking a deep breath, the severity of the situation settled in. This wasn't the time for fighting or getting upset with Alex. This was the time to make a plan and work for redemption. "I think the more important question we need to ask is how do we prove it and get our grade back," she whispered.

Ivy looked at her watch. 7:15. She sat on the wooden slate bench that faced her locker, her first time coming to the bay since school had begun. In the quiet aftermath of the science fair, after the gossip and whispers had circulated pointing fingers at her for being unstable and jealous enough to destroy their project, the only place that felt safe was the one place where bodies wouldn't be moving through. They'd be in the gymnasium, the atrium, and the pickup and drop off, but only a loser like her would be out in the hallways.

When no one was around, the vast empty halls were oddly quite comforting. She expected the school to be unsettling, maybe even creepy. There were collections of stories that floated around about hauntings. One brick-layer fell off the scaffolding and died during the expansion of the atrium. One year, a senior got drunk during prank week and fell off the catwalk in the auditorium, splitting his head open on the ground. There was the peanut allergy in the cafeteria, and most tragically, the scuba tank prank gone wrong in water sports. Come to think of it, her school seemed to be a magnet for tragedy.

A loud thump echoed behind her, causing her to shoot up. Every inch of her body was standing on edge, and she quickly snapped around to face her would-be phantom assaulter. She didn't find herself face to face with a ghost, a witch, demon, or vampire, but something much worse. Leslie Strafford, in the flesh.

"Hey," Leslie greeted somewhat shyly. "Um, are you lost? Do you need to call someone?" she asked, offering her phone, decked out in golden glitter.

"No. I just wanted to see my locker for the first time without it being surrounded by a bunch of poltergeists," Ivy said.

Leslie looked shocked. "You're locker 1234? We were wondering who that belonged to. It's not likely that they missed such prime locker real estate when dishing out the new assignments."

"Well, do you know anyone who wants it? I'm sure not going to put it to much use."

The girls looked at each other, trying to make sense of what exactly the other wanted, why exactly they were communicating, and if there was any small sliver of a reason to continue this interaction.

"I know you didn't destroy your project," Leslie finally spoke up, breaking the silence. "I think I can even get proof. Courtney never does anything without a trophy photo for her personal collection of what she considers achievements. And, you know, the gymnasium was full of people taking photos and videos. I bet if we collected these, we'd see her doing this in the background of one of them." She paused. "I can help you with this if you want."

Ivy hesitated. Should she trust the enemy? Was this a trap that was being carefully laid out to ensure she would spend the rest of the year in detention and be the laughing stock of the town when she was held back? Something was fishy. Not only was this too easy, the entire scenario, while plausible, was too convenient.

"Listen," Leslie interrupted, shattering Ivy's intense inner dialogue. "I know this is an unlikely conversation. But, if I can be completely honest, Courtney has to be stopped. She's like a disease. I probably shouldn't say this," she whispered," but most of them are." Ivy cocked her head, her interest piqued. "They only like me because my dad's rich, but they don't know we weren't always like this. My dad came from nothing, and my mom didn't even have a high school diploma. They got married because I showed up. Before we moved here, well, we weren't that much different than you. Dad just got a really good job after he finally had a research breakthrough, and sort of, well, lost it. He felt like he had to make up for everything. He started working out, buying expensive things, and he just changed. I don't think I actually like him like this, that's the funny part."

"I understand. I lost my dad," Ivy replied.

"That's right. Wow. Do you ever wonder if other people have it this way, or if somewhere out there, life is easy and free of complications for someone?"

"Leslie, is your life really that hard? Sure, you came from nowhere, but look at where you are now. I can't believe that you of all people are sitting here throwing a pity party."

"Says the queen of throwing pity parties. Come on, Ivy, you can't really be this mean to everyone all the time. Did you ever stop to think that if you maybe smiled once in a while or didn't bite everyone's head off all the time that maybe things would be a little easier for you?"

Ivy gasped. She sat on the bench, shocked, that this girl dared to turn around and place the blame back on her. Besides, it wasn't her job to be nice to anyone, and she didn't owe anyone a thing. People get what they give.

"I mean, people get what they give," Leslie continued. "Maybe if you just tried saying, 'Hello,' once in a while, you'd find out we're not that bad. You do make yourself an easy target for the group. If you quit giving people the power to react to you how they do, maybe they wouldn't go around smashing your science fair project."

Frantically searching for the right words, Ivy came up empty. She was digesting the very words she often used as a defense mechanism, served right back to her as advice. There was nothing more that she wanted than to be angry, frustrated, and vindicated. And yet, at the same time, she did realize she exuded a very firm and aggressive exterior. This was just the way life had shown her to be, one of the many lies she told herself as an excuse to support her lack of desire to change.

"Do you think anyone would believe us even if we did have proof?" she finally whispered, looking at her big toe wiggling under the thin canvas of her white sneakers. "I could probably bring them video and photos, and they'd still tell me I was wrong."

"See," Leslie jumped, "that's the exact attitude I'm talking about! Why would they blame you if you had the proof? You just want to think they'll blame you, so you don't have to try. That's what this is all about. You don't want to try. You don't want to try to be nice, to make friends, or to defend yourself. For fuck's sake, Ivy, at least defend yourself some time."

The sound of rubber shoes quickly tapping on the ceramic tile floor broke their awkward conversation. Both girls craned backward to try and see who was running down the hallway. The overhead fluorescent lights flickered, casting shadows and giving the darkened form a strobe-like effect as it approached.

"Please don't let it be a ghost, please don't let it be a ghost," Leslie whispered, her hands visibly shaking.

"I'm too young to die today," Ivy replied with a nervous laugh. "This school is too freaky, and I promise, oh hallway ghost, if you just let us go tonight, I will never step foot in here after hours again."

"Who needs to let you go?" Alex called, breaking out from the flickering shadows, breathing heavily. "I've been running all over this school looking for you. That's the theme of today, it seems. Run after your annoying ass. Your friend, Magnus, he's here to pick you up, but no one could find you."

"People are looking for me?" she gasped.

"Believe it or not, Ivy, there are people in the world who want to make sure you get home safely. Why is everything so damn difficult with you?"

"Everything...you know what? Nevermind. That isn't what's important right now. What is important is that Leslie saw Courtney ruining our project, and she's pretty sure if we try hard enough, we can find the video and social proof to take her down. We can get out of this, Alex!"

"I've already talked to Mr. Green. I told him that it had to be an accident and someone was probably too scared to own up to ruining our project. He agreed because you put so much time into the board, and it looked so good, that it didn't make sense for you to sabotage our own project. Luckily, he made the rounds before everything went to hell, and had already graded our research and presentation. We're going to be fine, Ivy."

"But, Alex, that's not the point. The point is that someone purposely destroyed our project and tried to ruin our chances. They need to be held accountable," she snarled. "I am not going to let this go. Courtney needs to be handled."

"And then what? Get her suspended, or expelled? Ruin her for validation? We are okay, and that's what matters," he replied.

"That is not what matters," Ivy exclaimed, her voice reaching a new height of squeakiness that she had previously never heard. "What matters is defending our position. People can't keep doing this to me and getting away with it!"

"Ah, there it is." Alex threw his hands up with a satisfied smirk on his face that screamed, 'I told you so.' "People can't keep doing this to you. News flash, Ivy, you're not a victim, and you're not the only person in the world. Sometimes you have to pick your battles and choose your outcome. We are okay. Our position is okay. That girl will get what's coming to her in due time, but when we weigh our options, we need to see how big the fight is that we're creating. You want to open an uphill marathon for a flat land 5k."

"I have no idea what that means."

"It means you're creating a bigger problem out of nothing," Leslie chimed in, placing her palm on Ivy's back and rubbing her reassuringly. "You're going to be okay, just breath, and relax."

"Relax?" she squealed. "You just told me to fight for myself, and now you're telling me to let it go. I'm not a victim, you say, but you're also clearly saying that I don't deserve too much effort."

"No, that's not what we're saying at all," Alex replied. "You should defend yourself, but you also need to see the big picture sometimes before you tape on your boxing gloves.

You're running around life with a brick hidden on your knuckles, waiting for the right chance to punch, instead of learning how to play the game and outsmart your opponent. Life isn't about one shiny moment of glory that will quickly fade. It's about endurance and making sure you're the last man standing when that bell chimes for the ninth round."

"Enough with your stupid sports analogies," she said, jumping to her feet. "You didn't even apologize for blaming me!"

"Well, you still haven't apologized for your jokes or mocking my parent's 'black names' to their face," he yelled back, over exaggerating the air quotes he placed on black names.

"You're too damn sensitive, and you're making your own mountain climb out of one flight of stairs. Fuck you, Alex. I didn't think you'd be one to let the truth slide by, but here you are. Still chasing the great and powerful asses of those kids," she yelled, pointing towards Leslie whose mouth was agape. "No matter what happens in this school, you will still bow down and kiss the feet of the rich kids, because that's where you belong and you don't want to mess up the power dynamic."

"Actually, that's not it at all. For someone who thinks they're so poor, you are so damn spoiled. You're only poor in your mind, Ivy. Your poverty sits up here," he spat, tapping the side of his forehead with his index finger.

"You know what? I don't need this. You don't know me. But I know you, and you," she said, pointing towards Leslie. "Keep your photos, your videos, your stories, your excuses, and your fake friendly moments. Just keep it all far away from me."

Ripping her backpack from the bench, she took off running down the dark, creepy hallway, through the flickering lights, into the shadows that would eventually wind their way back towards the atrium, and hopefully, to Magnus.

CHAPTER NINE

"*I*vy, Sweetheart, are you sure you don't want to go to the doctor?" her mother called from the other side of her bedroom door, gently jiggling the door handle to triple check her daughter still tightly locked in her bedroom. "I bought some soup just in case. They had that Campbell's on sale, 11 for $10. A good deal, yeah? I forgot how good soup was! Anyway, there's a bowl of noodle and vegetable outside your door. You might want to eat it before it gets too cold."

The heavy down blanket wrapped around her body was warm to the point of suffocation. Even though she had sweat dripping down her forehead, the confinement issued comfort and peace. She had spent the last week in bed, earbuds securely fastened in place, Netflix on steady streaming, and ignoring the world. She didn't want to see anyone, talk to anyone, and most of all, didn't want anyone to try and convince her she was the one who needed to change.

Once her mother's footsteps indicated she was safely out of contact range, Ivy quietly unlocked her bedroom door and hooked her fingers onto the aged aluminum tray that housed one bowl of soup, one sleeve of saltine crackers, one spoon, and two pieces of plain toast. The soup was still steaming, and she could feel the heat slowly drifting up when she bent over the full bowl to inhale the scent of the steamy comfort food.

A slight vibration noisily shook her bed; her phone was letting her know it still worked, and someone in the world wanted to talk to her. She flipped the silver plastic flap open to see forty-six missed calls, which was a shame because her phone would only show her the last twelve. Of course, if any of those calls were from someone other than Magnus, she'd be surprised.

"Voice mailbox full," she said with a laugh, thumbing through the old analog menu options. "There's a first time for everything, it seems."

Greedily slurping the salty soup, she began to make a mental list of all the ways she could make a living as a recluse. Luckily, in the internet age, the chance to work from a dark room without ever having to look another person in the face was becoming more probable. The only problem she could think of, well, list of problems, was that she didn't have a reliable computer, any idea of how to code, draw, use computer programs, social media, or any other skill that would allow her to be a recluse working online.

"It's all hopeless," she whispered, flopping back on her bed. "I'm absolutely hopeless."

"Not completely," Magnus chuckled, sliding into the room quietly. "Hey there, stranger. You finally forgot to lock the door."

"Damnit," she sighed. "I've done such a good job this week of making sure no one could get in."

"I know. You did an outstanding job, but even Rome fell eventually. Okay, champ. Why are you hiding?"

"I'm not hiding," she said, arms crossed, eyes averted. "I'm sick."

"Oh, like hell, Ivy. I can stay here all day. Come to think of it, I can stay here all weekend. I'm not leaving until we sort something out. The quicker you open your mouth and get some words out, the quicker we're going to start making progress. Enough. Let's go."

Ivy huffed and shook her head furiously. Her eyebrows were tightly stitched together, flowing into each other like a giant caterpillar making its way over her forehead.

"Okay, fine. Since you won't say it, I will. You're upset because you don't want to hear people challenging the bubble you've built around yourself. I know what happened in the locker bay, Ivy I think we have a lot to talk about. Where do you want to start?"

"Mag, this is so stupid. Everyone is making such a big deal out of something so tiny. It's been months now, can't everyone just let it go?" She pulled the blanket over her head and groaned, hoping this sent the signal that the conversation was over.

She failed.

"We can start right there. How do you want to do this? Do you want to talk about Alex's feelings, or why he may be...no, has a right to be upset over your joke?"

"Why are you doing this to me?" she screeched. "I haven't bothered you, or anyone, this week. I just want to lay in my bed, watch movies, and ignore all of you perfect people."

Magnus chuckled. Ivy had always been a fighter, a little bit scrappy, and one to fight back harder when she felt threatened.

"Ivy, sweets, talk to me," he whispered, moving the tray of half-eaten soup to the floor and snuggling next to her on top of the blanket she pulled even tighter. "I can tell you're really upset. Let's work through."

"What's there to figure out? People keep trying to get me to figure things out, and clearly, I'm not capable of understanding." She huffed, threw, the blanket off of her head and embraced his hug.

"Can we talk about what happened now? Maybe even just one small part? We don't have to tackle every situation at once."

"I really don't understand, Mag. I mean, a joke started all

of this. A stupid joke," she said, tears once again filling the corners of her eyes. The tears she rarely felt before this year threatened to make yet another appearance. "I'm about to cry again. I'm starting to think I need to see a doctor. I've never cried so much, I've never been so confused, and I've never felt so stupid."

"That's okay. Crying is okay. Being confused is okay," Magnus assured her, gently running his fingers over hers and up her forearms. "If you want to talk to someone, or feel that you need to, that's also okay. What isn't okay is thinking it's your job and your job alone to figure everything out and be perfect in this weird world."

Ivy sniffled and nodded her head slowly. "The joke?" she whispered.

"Are you sure you're feeling up for this?" he asked. She nodded, giving the okay. "I think we should start with Alex in general. He just had his life uprooted, everything he knew changed, and he's no longer in his ritzy Chicago private school but in a small town Indiana public school where everyone thinks they're somebody because they're small town rich. That's a big change in itself, but now he's also the only obvious non-white kid. Every single person who has ever had a joke, or question, or stereotype in their mind now thinks they have the opportunity to dump all of these on to him."

Ivy replied. "That's probably frustrating."

"I'm sure it is. Now try to think of all the stupid things people are saying to him, every single day. The kid can't catch a break or a moment of silence."

"But if everyone is doing it, why is he so mad at me?"

"He spends a lot of time with you in chem. His grade is based on your partnership, and he has to interact with you. For the sake of his grade and getting out of a class he doesn't belong in, no offense, he has to interact with you. You started off telling a joke that rightfully offended him, and he has to prepare himself to deal with that ignorance every single day, or to stand his ground and set boundaries immediately. He has the right to protect his own sanity."

"I agree," she whispered. "But...was the joke that bad?"

"Yes," he answered without hesitation. "Listen, we're really lucky, but we're also really sheltered. For us, slavery, civil rights, racism, they're just discussions in class, or online. When have you ever experienced being followed, accused of being in the wrong neighborhood, pulled over by police, or even rejected service just because you're white?"

"Never, of course."

"Exactly. We never see anything to support classroom discussions in real life. We aren't able to actually compare the meaning of these jokes to what people really do go through. Everyone in the world has a different journey, path, and history. Some people have walked a challenging path, generation after generation.

"Slavery is often softened, so people don't get offended, or even have to face their history. It's easy to crack a joke about picking cotton because picking cotton seems innocent. Right? We all know slavery is connected to picking cotton and agriculture."

"Everyone worked back then, Mag. It wasn't the luxurious life we have now. Plenty of white farmers picked cotton, too."

Magnus took a deep breath. "Sure. But slaves worked long days, often without food or water, in extreme weather. If they didn't meet goals, or maybe if they just looked in the wrong direction at the wrong time, they were beaten, starved, locked in small boxes in the ground that were like heat chambers, whipped, and a lot of times, killed. Women were raped by their masters, kids were stolen and sold, families ripped apart, and their very basic identities were wiped clean. These people had their names changed and were denied the right to even speak their home language. I can't even begin to touch on everything, or the horrors, or the pain that generation after generation went through."

"Oh, no," Ivy gasped. "I made a comment about his mom and dad having black names the night we did the research for our science experiment."

"Oh, Ivy. There's a lot of unresolved emotions and representation, history, and social stigma that people of color have to deal with daily, especially because certain groups of people don't accept ethnic sounding names."

"I don't like that you called the farmers masters. That sounds really bad, almost scary."

"We could call them owners. They owned people. Alex's ancestors most likely were considered property. To your ancestors, they were the same as donkeys, horses, dogs, or even rats."

"Well, that sounds even worse. Just because I'm white doesn't mean I have anything to do with slavery, though. That's not fair. I've heard of good plantations," she snapped.

"You have? Where? You might not have any blood ties, and no one is holding you personally responsible for what happened, but people are asking you to be responsible for your own education and understanding."

Ivy paused. The realization she based a lot of her social education on Hollywood representation settled in. She quieted.

"I've been telling these jokes for as long as I can remember. They always felt so normal."

"Have you ever told them to another person of color before?" he asked.

"Well, of course not. When would I have the chance?"

"Then when he told you what you said was offensive, since he is a person of color, why did you fight him? Why did you tell him what you said wasn't wrong?"

"I don't know. I haven't thought about it because I've been so mad," she whispered. "It was just a joke, and I assumed jokes are jokes regardless of who you are as a person."

"Put yourself in Alex's shoes. Can you imagine dealing

with this every day, all the time? He must be drained, having to explain jokes or talk about why there is no one specific representation of a black person, or why he should just be allowed to live. We haven't even talked about events that happened not so long ago, like segregation and Jim Crow. It's not all about slavery."

"Mag," she said, nuzzling into his shoulder. "How did you get so smart?"

He paused, letting the air steady between them. "My other grandma was black. When she died, my dad banned us from acknowledging that side of our family. For us, it was as simple as making a choice. I've started reading more lately, trying to figure out who I am and why my dad tried so hard to hide this part of us. It's hard. I still don't know why. Grams won't talk about it with me."

"What about all those times I cracked jokes with you?" Ivy paused, realizing Magnus never responded to her jokes dealing with race. She always assumed he either didn't get the joke or just didn't find it funny, but now she's seeing he felt he had to protect himself while also protecting their future. Unknowingly, she had put him in the position to make a choice between who he is and what their friend-ship means. She vowed to never do that to him again. "Hey, Mag?"

"Yup?"

"Can you drive me to Alex's house? I think I need to talk to him."

"Absolutely. But, Ivy," he laughed, "don't you want to shower first?"

The grand hollow chimes sounded out, filling the expan-sive foyer, sending chills down Ivy's arms and spine once again. The sound was nothing short of majestic; a loud, soul-filling, inspiring chime that warmed your body. She imagined the great churches of Europe warmed the small winding cobblestone paths with chimes just like these.

"Mag, are you okay?" she asked, anxiously teetering between her two feet and peering through the glass doors, hoping to see someone coming to answer their unannounced visit. "You don't have to stay with me. I'll understand."

"No. It's fine. You may need some help with this, and if anyone can keep you on the subject or help you out, it's me. I'm not going to do this for you, though."

"I know. Thank you... And, Mag?"

"Yes?"

"What do you think about us going somewhere? Trying to find a way to save some money, going somewhere far far away that has food we've never tried, languages we've never heard, and colors we've never seen?"

"Wow. What happened to you in your room last week?" he laughed, pulled out of his surprise by the soft clicks of stiletto shoes coming towards the door.

Ivy snapped her head towards the door, her stomach tightened. A wave of uncertainty flooded her. She just hoped she didn't vomit on those expensive looking black shoes standing on the other side of the glass door.

Locking eyes with Alex's mom, she lifted her hand and gave a soft wave. She tried her best to issue a sincere, genuine smile, but doing so was one of the most difficult activities she had ever consciously endured. A deep sigh of relief slipped from her tightly sewed lips when Leticia unlocked the door and cracked it open.

"Good evening," she said, her body tense. "Can I help you?"

"Good evening, Ma'am. I, um, first of all, I'm sorry to come unannounced. Alex didn't answer his phone. I...I wanted to talk to Alex, but since you're also here, maybe you, too," she said quietly, shifting her gaze to her sneakers.

"We're just about to sit down for dinner," she replied. Ivy nodded, her eyes still on her toes, and turned to walk away. "But you and your friend are welcome to join us. Come in."

Ivy heard Magnus release a deep breath as the door opened wider, welcoming them inside. "Are you okay?" she whispered, grabbing his hand and giving it a soft squeeze. When he nodded in return, she did her best to issue a soft and supportive smile. She wasn't sure how much of a support system she could be for her friend when she needed him to be hers.

"Alex," Leticia called through the expanse as they rounded the foot of the staircase leading to the second story and approached the large eat-in kitchen. "Can you put two more place settings down, please?"

"Oh, no, Ma'am. We don't need to eat. We don't want to interrupt. I can make this quick so you can get back to your dinner," Ivy assured.

"Don't be silly. Join us. Conversations are often best over a good meal where you can warm your stomach, your mind, and your friends. Besides, Demetrius is at a training camp, and we have plenty of food for all of us."

Dishes clinked together, accompanied by the gentle metal tinkering of silverware being jostled around. Stepping into the kitchen, they were met with a loud gasp followed by Alex letting the heavy silverware slip from his hands and clatter loudly on the ceramic floor. His jaw fell open, and he paused in his tracks, assessing the unexpected visitors who now invaded his safe space.

"What is this? What are they doing here?" he asked.

Leticia nodded and opened her arms towards the duo. "We're having dinner guests. Your friend, Iris, was it?"

"Ivy," she corrected shyly.

"Ivy tried to call you but felt strongly enough about needing to talk she decided to drop by. I invited them to stay for dinner. Now, what would you two like to drink?"

"Water," they answered in unison while being ushered towards the round table tucked into a luscious corner window, bordered by a plush booth and soft velvety pillows.

The table was quickly filled with a skillfully carved roasted chicken, candied carrots, steamed broccoli, and a crisp salad loaded with vegetables and an exotic crumbly white creamy cheese. The bowls and platters that housed the simple delicacies were bright and bold, elegantly patterned with vibrant geometric designs, reminding Ivy of their many lessons on Greek mythology.

Ivy watched her hosts closely, mimicking their actions. When they unfolded the emerald green napkins embroidered with flowers and initials in the corner, placing the thick fabric into their laps, she did the same. When they adjusted their silverware to perfect spacing, she followed suit. She straightened her back and found herself pleased at displaying the best posture she'd used in quite some time, fighting through the growing burn that sprouted in her shoulders.

"What was it you wanted to talk about," Alex asked, holding out the bowl containing the carrots and nodding his head to ask if they wanted some for their own plate.

"Yes, please," Ivy replied. "I, well, I'm sorry Alex. I'm not sure how to do this or talk about this. I've never had to do anything like this before," she said, fidgeting with the edges of her napkin and running her fingers over the raised threads that created beautiful flowers. "I was talking to Magnus about everything that's happened since you've been here. And I wanted to tell you that I'm really, really sorry. I know it may not mean much, and I know it's not an excuse that I didn't know better, but I think I do now."

The room was still; not even the slightest movement was made towards any of the delicious food spread out before the hungry dinner attendees. The room was tense and heavy, but Ivy knew she had to continue. She turned to Alex's mother to continue.

"And I'm really, really sorry that I insinuated your name was anything other than a beautiful name. I'm ashamed of myself. There was a lot I didn't know, like how on slave ships people were denied their names, or the ability to speak their own language. We don't get first-hand experience or education with people that aren't...well...white."

"I understand," Leticia replied. "And I do appreciate your recognition and bravery in coming to my house to tell me as such."

"Yes," Alex replied softly. "Thank you."

"So, this happens to you quite a bit?" Ivy asked. "I mean, you have to deal with people like me a lot?"

"Every day," Leticia began. "Every single day. Even as a doctor, I have to deal with patients commenting on my name, asking to see my credentials, trying to quiz me on medical knowledge, or just being surprised that a black female is their specialist."

"What do you say to them?" Ivy replied.

"Nothing. You get to a point in your life where you no longer have the energy to spend every waking moment of your day telling people basic pieces of respect and communication. I used to try, to explain why what was being said was done in bad manners. Nine times out of ten, I'd get some sort of return that I was too sensitive or the rude one. We learn to live our life so we don't lose every day to someone else. You can't fight everyone."

"You've seen that with me," Alex continued. "The boys want me on this team and that team. They're interested in me because they think I'm an athlete, not because of anything else I have to offer. I didn't even realize this happened until we moved here. I always thought my mom was just overdramatic," he chuckled, " but living here has been a learning experience for me, too."

"Yes, it has," Leticia responded. "Did you know my name is actually Latin? My name was popular in medieval England and is a synonym for happiness in Spanish. They even have a saint named Leticia in Spain, so it's a common name and has nothing to do with "being black."

"I am so sorry," Ivy interrupted, gasping.

"Do you know why you had those predisposed notions about my name?"

"Maybe TV? Or the people around me? It's not a name I hear that often, or when I do hear it, it's a black...colored (replace with African American?)...um..."

"Black is fine," she replied. "I'm proud to be a black woman. Demetrius is proud to be a black man. Interesting, isn't it? That something so beautiful can be tainted just by how society views a person based on their skin color.

Ivy hung her head, trying to hide the burning sensation in her cheeks. This is what shame feels like, she told herself. She thought this talk would go differently. In her head, she'd walk up to the house, ring the doorbell, apologize, get a hug, and move on. But she sat here, at their dinner table, getting an education she was thankful for, and one that she felt deeply.

"Why are you taking the time to teach me?" she asked.

"You came to us, child. That doesn't always happen. I have the opportunity to open my home to you and help you change your views, maybe even my son's future. I could have shut my door and shut your mind. We have to pick and choose our battles. I think you are a battlefield we can play on."

The conversation was interrupted by a soft gulping choke that erupted from the corner of the booth. "I'm sorry," Magnus said, wiping a tear from his eye. "Keep talking." He softly sobbed, trying his best to bite his lip and keep the words and sounds tucked tightly inside.

"Oh, Magnus," Ivy sighed. "Is it too much? If you want to go, I can order an Uber or walk to meet you somewhere." She laid her hand on his knee, feeling his legs trembling under the soft weight of her hand. She knew they were seconds away from a breakdown. "Magnus used to live here," she whispered. "Not the people you bought it from, but the people before that."

"I see," Leticia responded. "The house must have some strong memories for you. A good house tends to do that."

"I was sitting right here when they told me my parents died," he choked out. "Right here."

Leticia's smile quickly faded to a look of motherly horror. She slid over and embraced the sobbing teenager who was quickly melting into the little boy who lost his life in that same spot years before. She offered her condolences and rocked him softly, one hand on his cheek, the other around his back and rubbing his shoulder.

"You smell like my grandmother," he sighed. "She used to hold me like this when I was upset, and she always smelled like her bubble bath."

"Chanel Number Five Velvet Milk," they replied in unison. A soft giggle came from both, Ivy watched Magnus deeply inhale and find calm in the arms of a woman who was a stranger only a few moments ago.

"I'm sorry," he apologized. "I didn't mean to interrupt you. I knew I had to come for Ivy because she can be stubborn, and sometimes as socially blind as a barn bat, but she's a good girl. She is."

"You're allowed to cry around here," Alex said. " I'm sorry you have to remember such a horrible time. Should we skip dinner and just move right to ice cream?" he laughed, the other members of the table joining in.

"Is there anything that you want to ask me, or Alex?" Leticia offered, shooting down the ice cream for dinner suggestion and placing large slices of chicken on everyone's plate. With a nod commanding the teenagers to start eating, the type of nod only a mother can deliver, she continued. "You're welcome to open any subject with us if doing so will help you in your journey."

"I'm not even sure what I might need to ask...but if I think of something later, can I email you?" she asked.

"How about one better. You can call me. Any time. But Ivy, please remember." She looked at Ivy sternly, and her gaze was met with an understanding and curious nod. "You can joke about humanity as a whole or choices people make, but when you start breaking down jokes into characteristics people are born with, you're teaching people they are born inferior, or what they cannot control is a piece of shame. I'm going to give you a book to take home. I want you to read it and then come over one day for tea to talk again."

"Okay," Ivy agreed. "I can do that."

CHAPTER TEN

*E*agerly flipping the pages, Ivy made her way through Toni Morrison's *The Bluest Eye* for the second time. She wanted to sit down and have a meaningful conversation with Leticia when she finally picked up the phone to schedule tea. Finals and term papers had delayed her progress and stolen her focus, but having Alex for a Chemistry partner was definitely a stroke of luck. The school refused to move him at midterms, despite there being four kids who dropped out of AP Chemistry Two, and Alex passing the entrance test. Rumors had it that a storm was brewing and the school was about to get a major lesson in just how strong of a woman Alex's mother was.

Ivy found herself growing attached to Leticia, and for the first time, she felt what life was like with a mother who doted on you and tried to lift you up to a better standing in your life. She could tell her own mother was trying, and their relationship was continually improving, but Leticia didn't have to try. When it came to being a mother, she just was. Whenever there was a Chemistry paper to write or an experiment to finish or report to formulate, they would meet up at Alex's – Magnus included. Returning to the house had become a sort of therapy, and he found himself releasing the pain he had internalized for years. Frustration and anger dissipated, and with every entry into the house that should have been his, he became okay with where his future might lead and more understanding of why his grandmother forced the sale of his house.

During paper breaks, even though she was tired and drained from saving brains and creating groundbreaking treatments, Leticia taught Ivy how to make peach ice tea without the yellow canned powder, knead bread, make soup broth, plant rose bushes, sew a button back into place, and even how to create strong but delicate braid to keep her hair in place during windy, stormy spring days. She showed Ivy how to do an at-home manicure during the writing of a paper on the periodic table of elements, and she taught her how to walk in high heels during an experiment on chemical reactions between everyday household products.

Alex took a little more time to open back up. Ivy didn't mind; she saw he also closed himself off from most of their classmates. Initially, she was confused by why he didn't immediately open up to her like his mother, or why he didn't seem excited to teach her or work with her. At school, she heard the jabs, saw the teasing pokes, watched the way the boys tried to interact by suddenly becoming historians on black athletes, or how they changed the way they talked when Alex came by.

With each passing day, she found herself growing more and more tired of her classmates' antics. She really recognized the ignorance behind her first interaction with Alex, like a heavy load of bricks being dropped off the tenth story and directly on her head. The impact stayed heavy on her mind. But with that realization came one more she wasn't ready for: she had no idea what to do or how to address her fellow students. For one, she felt below them. They had no reason to listen to her, and they believed they had no reason to listen to her. She still wasn't sure what her role was and how to discuss her concerns with her perceived enemies without stepping on the toes of a delicate relationship, perhaps the only friendly relationship she's had outside of Magnus.

Many times, she was tempted to talk to the boys in her class like they walked straight out of Deliverance, usher them into the classroom with a recording of 'Dueling Banjos,' and quote ridiculous movies featuring a cast of good ol' boys. Sadly, she knew the purpose would be lost on them, but if she ever had to do another science fair experiment, she definitely wanted to focus on the way people interact with each other based on perceived notions and first visual impressions.

Even now, she couldn't understand why Alex went ahead and tried out for the basketball team. Or why he was so excited or surprised when he did make the team. Or why he continued to put up with the attitudes and jabbing of the boys when she knew how that really made him feel.

"Earth to Ivy," her mom called, gently extending her leg down the center of the couch and playfully kicking her thigh. "What in the world are you reading? It's one of those boy books, isn't it? That one that teaches you all that sexy stuff with whips, ay?" she teased.

"Ew, gross! No, and even if it were, I wouldn't admit to you! You're my mom," she groaned. "Besides, we all know Magnus doesn't like girls, so who in the world would I be reading a book like that to try and impress?"

"Well, what are you reading? Do you think it's something I might like?"

Ivy paused, cocking her head and looking at her mother quizzically. "I've never seen you read anything before. I'm not sure." She hesitated, looking at the cover of her book, running her thumbs over the interior pages that she had highlighted, underlined, and tabbed. "You know, this one's for school. I'm not sure that you'd like it. But, if you want, I'm kind of enjoying this reading thing. Maybe we could go to the library and look around for something to read and discuss...together?" she suggested.

"Nah, that's okay." Her mom sighed. "I don't really like to read, anyway. Well, unless it's something telling me about what the glitzy glamourpusses in Hollywood are doing." She excused herself, heading off to the kitchen to futz around in the cabinets. Her new favorite hobby was to rearrange the few items they did own, wipe down the counters, and mop the floors. The pine-scented liquid became her new alcohol, and Ivy had zero complaints about this.

A sharp four staccato rap tinkered off the front door.

"Mags," she exclaimed, bounding to the door, eagerly ripping the door open and pulling Magnus inside. "Whatcha doing?"

"You're in a good mood today," he gasped, teetering on his feet from the force of the pull. "I brought prom magazines. I thought we could drink some tea and look at all the dresses to help plan for Homecoming."

"Ooh, tea. How very bougie of you," she mocked, and then sighed. "But I'm not sure I want to go to Homecoming. It's so fancy, and everyone will be rubbing it in our faces how they have someone special, and we're just there, alone."

"We're not alone. We'll have each other," he replied. "Or was there someone special that you were hoping would ask you?"

"No, no one," she quickly stammered, turning around and heading into the kitchen. "Mom, do we even have tea? Like real tea, in the bags."

"We do, actually. I have a box for when I get a sore throat. Top shelf, next to the Cheerios," she replied.

"Cheerios, Cheerios," she hummed, fishing through the cabinets until she found the famous yellow box and the small green one next to it containing the teabags. She grabbed two mismatched mugs adorned with faded teddy bears, hearts, and sweet sayings, swiftly filled them with tap water, and tossed them in the microwave.

"What in the hell are you doing?" Magnus gasped. "You can't microwave the water. It's going to boil and blow up in your face. Well, that's what YouTube says, but in the very least, it's not going to taste good. You have to control the water to get a good flavor, and you sure don't want a hot ceramic mug. Don't you have a kettle?"

"I barely knew we had tea," Ivy answered, astonished. "I also didn't know tea was so hard to make. Sheesh, thank goodness I'm not British."

Magnus dug around in the kitchen cabinets, finding a decent soup pan. After transferring the water to the slightly dented vessel, he placed it on the lit gas stove and patiently waited for the water to boil.

"I heard salt makes water boil faster," Ivy said, proud of this nugget of cooking wisdom.

"Girl. Saltwater tea? Are you out of your mind?" Magnus laughed, shaking his head and jostling her shoulders. "If you ever want to be able to make it on your own, we're going to have to put you through some cooking classes or something. You worry me, girl."

"The sad thing is I've practically been on my own for most of my life," she sighed and broke out into a hearty laugh. "How did I ever survive without you? Now, toss me one of those magazines. Let's look at dresses and dream of being one of the pretty girls that will actually get a date."

"You'll get a date, Ivy You are one of the pretty ones. One of these days, I hope you'll see yourself for what you really are."

Ivy giggled and blushed, "You have to say that, Mag. You're my best friend. If you didn't say that, I'd have to kick your butt. Oh my gosh, look at this one," she gasped, pointing to one of the slick, glossy pages. The model was draped in a soft violet gown, the top half made of silk that seemed to shimmer slightly darker, almost blueish where it caught the light. The bust was ruched and fitted, moving into a bodice where the fabric was manipulated in a way that made it look like soft scales. The skirt flared out in a series of elaborate godets, hugging the hips in layers of bright purple chiffon until it blossomed like an upside down spring lilly. The hips were coffered in layers of delicate petals, raining down the skirt as if someone was standing over the model, dropping the tiny flowers onto the dress. "This is the most beautiful gown I have ever seen." She sighed, eagerly reading the dress description to find the designer and purchasing information.

"It's a Bérenger," Magnus replied, finally spotting the designer's name in the fine print. "Absolutely beautiful and a bargain at the low price of $8,000, your left ovary, and the first three kids you manage to pump out of your right."

"Isn't this a prom catalog? What is this, prom for royalty and bank robbers?"

The duo broke out in hearty laughter, sipping their cups of tea that would make the entire United Kingdom cringe, and scanned each page, creating backstories in fake British accents for each model. On and on they carried until the only logical story that remained was the girl who bought a lucky lottery ticket, buying the dress to impress her crush, and then realizing she's better off alone because she's too young to be tied down.

"And we end the stack of magazines on my own personal story. I'll be right back. I'm off to buy a lottery ticket and my dream gown," she joked. "Who are you going to ask, Mag? If you go, that is. Anyone special?"

"There's someone I'm thinking about asking. I don't like rejection, though. I'm not even sure I'd know how to ask them."

"Well, even though I want to be asked by someone, I don't think that's going to happen for me. If your person rejects you, which they'll be a fool for doing, we can go together! Let's make a promise to be each other's last resort until we die."

Magnus furrowed his brow, not quite reacting how Ivy anticipated. "I guess," he said. "That seems kind of harsh, though."

"Oh lighten up. I don't really expect you to be around

until I die. It'd be nice to be friends forever, but I won't force you to be stuck to my side that long. I wouldn't wish that curse on you."

A soft chime cut through the possible realization that they would either be alone forever or risk being stuck together, providing some much-needed relief.

"It's Alex," Magnus said, sliding his fingers over the cool glass screen of his fancy smartphone. "They won their game. Everyone is going to a house party, but he doesn't want to go. He's inviting us over for a movie marathon."

"Sounds great," Ivy beamed.

"Yup. Great," Magnus sighed in reply, scooting the magazines back into a nice even stack.

The expansive basement hid what felt like a multitude of rooms. Ivy marveled at each open door: a gym worthy of a luxurious hotel, a wooden spa sent from Finland, a room built for entertaining that looked like an English pub, a craft room that looked like it hadn't actually created anything, and finally, a movie theater. The screen covered the entire front wall, and they all took places in large leather recliners, carefully placed in alternating rows on slight risers.

The air was coated in the thick saltiness of popcorn dripping with butter. Ivy eagerly dug her hands in her red and white striped plastic container, scraping the heavy oil from her fingertips against the thick scalloped edges.

"What do you think? The Indiana Jones trilogy or an 80s celebration? We could enjoy the classics of the Brat Pack," Alex said, sorting through the DVD collection while Magnus scanned through their digital files. "We could work our way through Harry Potter, too. Not all tonight, of course."

"Ooh, the Brat Pack," Magnus and Ivy said in unison.

"I had a feeling you guys would say that," Alex laughed. "Shall we start with Pretty in Pink, Sixteen Candles, or The Breakfast Club?"

"The Breakfast Club, without a doubt," Ivy sputtered. "Hey, A, do you have any soda? This popcorn is delicious, but the butter is so thick. I'm not sure water will wash it all the way down."

Alex popped the first DVD in, setting up the remainder of their night's viewing schedule in a neat stack. He ran his finger over a panel on the wall, pressing on the top right, releasing a small rectangular door with a click. The soft amber light that spilled forth revealed an empty cavern.

"Looks like the fridge is empty. I'll pop upstairs real quick. My parents don't drink a lot of pop. They'll probably have some Sprite, Ginger Ale, or flavored sparkling water. Any preference?"

"Flavored sparkling water. Might as well keep being all fancy since we've already had a tea party."

Alex nodded and took off upstairs, the opening credits drifting through the room from expensive foreign speakers with theater quality sound. The supple leather cradled Ivy and threatened to pull her to sleep before the movie made it to the first scene.

"These chairs are divine," Magnus cooed. "I'm not sure I'll even make it through the first movie, let alone an entire movie marathon."

"I know. It's like we're soaking into some Italian clouds and hanging over movie theater heaven. Now I understand why they don't put chairs like this in the theater. No one would watch the movie."

"Hey Ivy, why do you think Alex didn't go to the house party? It just doesn't make sense to me. Tonight was a big game, and there are all those silly traditions. I'm sure they have to go tip cows, bust mailboxes, throw patio furniture into pools and have a bunch of drunk hookups that will be in the rumor mill on Monday."

"Well, maybe that's not who he is," she replied, sitting up in her chair to face Magnus.

"I like the kid, but one day he's over here, the next he's

over there, and he can't just make up his mind who he wants to be. If you ask me, it's not fair to us. We're probably his only real friends. You know those other guys don't care about. They just like the idea of having a black friend."

"And you don't? What are you saying, Mag?" she asked, shaking her head.

The theater door swung open, promptly ending the conversation.

"You guys still awake?" Alex laughed. "Those chairs are killer."

"We were actually just talking about that," Ivy replied, reaching out to grab a can of sparkling orange water and a large cup of ice. "Thank you, my friend. You know, I think we should watch something a little cheesier and a bit more upbeat. Like Pretty In Pink. This one's too serious, and I have to be honest, I'm going to pass out in this chair."

"There are blankets in the consoles in between the seats if you need one. What do you think, Magnus? Should we change?"

"I think that sounds good. Why not watch a movie about a big school dance and a girl who wants something she can't have without realizing that's not what she needs?"

Alex stopped in his tracks, scanning Magnus quizzically. "Dude, you sound a little bitter. Are you having some dance date drama or something?"

"I guess you could say that," he angrily sighed. "Yeah, you absolutely could say that. I got rejected today, and I'm sure you guys know how that feels."

"That explains everything," Ivy exclaimed. "That's why you came over with the prom magazines and why you seem to have such a stick up your butt right now. Aha! Who was it Mag? Do we know them?"

"No," he growled. "You don't. I don't want to talk about me anymore. What about you Alex? What are your plans for homecoming?"

Ivy jumped to attention in her seat, the smooth leather

squeaking under the swift movement of her feet. There were rumors, of course, being whispered around the halls, locker bays, and bathrooms. She acted like she didn't hear them, or that she didn't care, but she clung to every syllable. She knew every name that had been traded in every classroom over the last two weeks.

Alex awkwardly laughed. "We don't have to talk about this, man. You know what? Maybe Pretty In Pink isn't the right movie for tonight. I'm thinking we just say to hell with it and make a field trip to Hogwarts."

Magnus refused to let down and pushed on forcefully. "Now, A, don't be shy. We're your friends. Surely there's someone you're asking or someone that you've already asked."

"Yeah, man. I, um, have a date. I've been hanging out with Leslie Strafford lately. She's a really cool girl. I asked her after practice this week. I'm pretty excited," he laughed.

Ivy's mouth fell open. Public enemy number one. Her mind. When did he have the time to hang out with her and how had she not noticed? Surely he would have said something or dropped some hint. He hadn't delivered even the most subtle indication that he had even a sliver of interest in Leslie.

"That's great, buddy," she choked. Her eyes met with Magnus, and she noticed the way they twinkled in the darkness. The corners of his mouth were slightly upturned into a satisfied smirk.

He already knew.

CHAPTER ELEVEN

*I*vy slipped in to the soft lilac chiffon gown and marveled at the way the fabric draped so perfectly around her body. Even though they had to buy polyester chiffon, not silk, and had to do their best with pre-made patterns that could be adapted, she felt they came pretty close to the dreamy Berengér dress of her dreams. Magnus' grandmother had happily jumped in to help, excited to have a stitching project that wasn't a hole in some socks, a loose thread on a table cloth, or a popped button. The chance to pull out her sewing machine and create something truly beautiful took years off her face, softening the creases life had added.

The duo spent countless hours cutting tiny petals and chiffon circles that they scrunched into little flowers. And, in the end, with very sore fingers from guiding the needles for days and days and calloused knuckles from where the scissors constantly rubbed while cutting, the dress was completed.

She didn't want to take away from the dress and opted to brush her hair back into a ponytail that was slightly teased at the crown with a subtle curl. She kept her makeup as basic as any other day, only adding a little more mascara and a darker matte nude lip.

"You look so elegant," Magnus sighed, watching her walk down the hallway towards the living room.

The gasp that escaped from her mother revalidated

that she was a showstopper in this gown. She was going to light up the atrium.

"I feel like a princess," she giggled. Deep joy was bubbling up, naturally kissing her skin with radiance, adding extra flecks of sparkle in her eyes, and easing the stress that was normally present on every word she spoke. "I didn't know you could feel like this. Or maybe I should say I didn't think those horrible Hollywood movies where the girl goes on and on about finally feeling beautiful were anything but hogwash, but I think they may have been on to something. I really do."

A soft rustling pulled Ivy's attention to her mother who was clumsily digging through the contents of her purse. Small bottles clanked together, empty gum wrappers rustled, and her oversized key ring jingled with its constant shifting. "Ah," she exclaimed, pulling out a small clear tube. "Okay, so it's not like an actual bottle, but a sample still smells the same," she said, cutting through the judgmental looks she created in her mind – the looks that were absolutely not happening in this room of people all too familiar with creative workarounds for every step in life.

Sliding towards Ivy, her shaking hands fumbled with the white ribbed plastic plug, eventually freeing it from the tight seal. A soft powdery fragrance erupted into the air and melted down until it settled as a lush floral bathed in citrus. A collective deep inhalation was followed by a sighing exhale.

"That smells so delicious," Ivy lulled. "Oh my goodness. I've never smelled anything so interesting!" Truthfully, she'd never smelled anything more than her deodorant, baby powder, and the occasional magazine page that hadn't already been rubbed off. The chance to wear real perfume, created for what she considered real women, filled her with pride.

"I have one more surprise for you," her mother said, beaming with excitement Ivy had never before seen. "It's this way. Come with me." She ushered the teens to the front door, swinging it open to reveal a gunmetal grey Kia Soul.

"Mom," Ivy gasped.

"Don't get too excited. It's just a rental for tonight. I tried to get you kids a limo, but that will have to wait for your senior prom. I do need to have it back by two tomorrow afternoon. And, they don't know you're driving it, so please don't scratch, dent, ding, or wreck the cute little thing. Okay?"

"Okay!" Magnus and Ivy exclaimed in unison.

Climbing inside, they looked at each other with child-like joy when the new car smell of vinyl, plastic floor coverings, and carpet hit their noses.

"You still smell better, but it's a close race," Magnus teased. "Oh, I forgot," he jumped, reaching across the car to collect a small box from his grandmother who had toddled outside. "I got you something." He smiled and slipped a lily corsage over Ivy's wrist. "Looks nice, just the perfect shade of purple."

"Yes, yes it does. Thank you so much, Mag," she replied, throwing her arms around his neck and giving him a peck on the cheek. She didn't notice the blush creeping up his neck, the gentle smile that formed, or the deep sigh that slowly exhaled when he put the car in drive. She twisted her wrist in the softly fading sunlight, admiring the details nature had painted upon the beautiful flower and then turned to wave goodbye to the women in the driveway sending them off to their first dance.

The excitement bubbled over during the three-mile drive to school. There were no concerns about what others might think about her dress, if anyone would notice her dancing, if any comments would be made about her coming with Magnus, or if her shoes really didn't go with her dress or were maybe a little too scuffed for such an elegant gown. Not a single negative thought remained in her mind. The moment she zipped the layers of smooth fabric against her skin, all doubt vanished and she became someone new. She felt confident, she oozed pride, and she stood a little taller.

"Oh, Mag," she gasped. "I forgot to tell you how dapper you look! The charcoal was an excellent decision. Your eyes are magnificent."

"Why, thank you, my queen. I quite like bucking the status quo myself. We're just two beautiful people tonight, aren't we?"

Laughter filled the interior, toppling over the music and intertwining with the beats of the bass drum pounding through the bottom speakers. If cloud nine was brought down to earth, Ivy was sure she was on her way to sit on its fluffy cushion.

They parked the car and bounced up the walkway to the atrium, mingling with fellow students, enjoying the ooh's from girls when they spied Ivy's magnificent custom dress. She would smile over her shoulder and wink, ignoring the eye rolls Magnus delivered. There were no questions, he was enjoying the attention as much as she was.

The double doors pushed open into a hallway of crepe paper streamers in the school's trademark blood red and ivory. Balloons filled the floor, bouncing with the softest touch from a passerby. Silver stars on curled strings hung from fishing line crisscrossed over the atrium ceiling, intermixed with fairy lights and long gathered strands of sheer fabric. Magic radiated and filled every pore on Ivy's body with potential.

But then they turned the corner towards the photo booth tucked into the auditorium. Posing for photos was a group of sixteen rowdy kids, joking and talking over each other, and giving the photographer hell as he desperately tried to put them into place to snap a photo he could sell their parents. And right in the center, arms locked tightly around each other, were Alex and Leslie.

"I thought he said they were coming alone, and that's why he didn't want to meet up or go to dinner?" Ivy said, her voice carrying a subtle tremble of betrayal.

"Yeah, that's what he said. But I think what he meant was he didn't want to bring us along."

Hours of drinking fruit punch and dancing your heart out without caring who was watching was an extremely efficient recipe for a sudden and intense bathroom break. Ivy dreaded the idea of cramming her way into the bathroom stall and trying to keep her beautiful gown off the floor, off the toilet, and hopefully, no stray layers getting accidentally misplaced. She read Teen Times every single month, like every other teen girl, and laughed at one too many embarrassing moment quotes. The potential for a disaster was heavily imprinted on her mind, and she was determined to not spend tomorrow penning her own world-ending moment that would haunt her for the rest of her life.

Knowing the main bathroom at the entrance to the atrium would be packed, she moved swiftly towards the large double doors leading to the cafeteria and then spun into the girl's locker room. Wasting no time, she scurried into the handicapped stall, thankful to see it open. For one, it was one of the only stalls in the entire school that had floor to ceiling partitions because it also included a shower for the students and their assistants. For another, she knew it was going to be one of the cleanest stalls because no one ever used it. Rumors circulated that the girls' locker room was haunted by the student who died in the scuba diving accident. Ivy was convinced one of the teachers started the rumor to cut down on post-gym truancy.

Relieving her bladder had never felt so good, and she enjoyed the opportunity to get off her feet as well. Wearing heels wasn't her forte, or specialty, or even a regular practice. The painful pin prickles that settled in her arch once she sat on the toilet caught her by surprise. She decided she was in no rush to return to the dance. Magnus would assume she was touching up her lipstick, fussing with her hair, or caught in line like a typical female making a pit stop. For once, the mystical time warp known as the ladies bathroom would work in her favor.

She gasped, throwing her hands over her mouth. Her stomach dropped when a chorus of voices cut through the silence of the empty locker room. She recognized the voices as they grew closer – the Super Six. Their laughter alone would make a hyena pass out from fright, and here she was, locked in the bathroom stall with them on the other side. At least the partition would keep her from being seen.

"Have you seen it yet?" one of the girls laughed, accompanied by a chorus of loud reciprocal giggles.

"Oh my God, Nat! No, I haven't."

Ivy recognized Leslie's voice immediately, and her hair stood on end.

"Come on. You said you were going to get in his pants and tell us if what they say is true. I'm interested to know what you think about it compared with Jackson's."

More laughter ensued with a gaggle of girls talking over each other. There wasn't enough space in between words to make anything out. "

"But stop being greedy, Leslie. Your dad is filthy rich. You don't need to try and lock down Alex. Let one of us try to get in that family line, one of us that are just rich, not dripping in loose dollar bills rich like you two."

"Yeah, I second that," another girl chimed in, laughing. Ivy knew these two voices but couldn't place them. "Can you imagine if he hadn't come? Thank God we finally have a black kid on the basketball team. There's no way we would have won without him. I mean, I'm not racist, but it seems like everything they say is true. Athletic – check. Confident – check. Sexy and smooth – check. Those muscles – check. Big penis – we'll know in the morning – check."

"You all are absolutely ridiculous," Ivy heard Leslie say.

"Does anyone want to raise their bet? We're up to $325,

and that's a good pair of sunglasses or a decent pair of shoes. I'm still assuming he's at least 8.5 and that Leslie won't be able to screw him because she can't handle that much man."

Ivy gasped, thankful their cackles and laughter flooded the bathroom and drowned out her shock. She tried her best to separate the chatter and hear more, but the group moved towards the exit, their gossip and vulgarity just becoming a distant murmur until it faded into the music creeping in from the atrium.

"What are you doing out here?" Magnus asked, concern scribbled over his forehead. "I've been looking everywhere for you. Are you sick? Was it the punch? Do you want to go home?"

"Woah, Mag," Ivy replied, her head spinning from the questions that became interlaced with her anger. She placed one hand on the cool curb, feeling the smoothness of the yellow paint where it abruptly stopped covering the rough and rocky concrete.

He took a seat next to her, careful to scoot the stray tulle layers of her skirt out of the way before stepping down. The anxiety radiating from her once happy body was palpable, vibrating in the space between them.

"Did I do something?" he solemnly asked.

"Oh, no. You didn't do anything. You're perfect, Mag. You're my best friend. You've made tonight better than I ever could have expected." She paused, took a deep breath, and then proceeded to tell him everything she overheard while locked in the haunted handicapped stall. The parking lot began to spin. She placed her forehead to her kneecaps to steady the dizziness.

"That's horrible," he whispered in return. "Absolutely horrible. Do you think we should tell him? Or would that also make us horrible people?"

Silence crept in between them, interrupted only by the occasional burst of music that erupted every time the atrium doors opened. Ivy slipped her hand into Magnus', finding relief in the comfort of familiarity. She gave his fingers a squeeze, and laid her forehead back down to her kneecaps, this time with Magnus' hand sandwiched in place.

"Do you think we'd be horrible for telling him?" she asked, speaking into his hand, the vibrations of her words tickling her face. "Or do you think he'd even believe us? I kind of feel like if we tell him, it won't go well. I feel like he has to figure this one out on his own, and that's hard Mag. That's so hard to think about."

"Why?"

"Because it's Alex. He's our friend. He's…Alex…"

"What does that mean, Ivy? Why are you letting this get to you like this? Do you think it's because you're jealous he didn't ask you to the dance?" he asked firmly, slipping his hand free with a quick pull.

Ivy shot up, not expecting that question and not entirely sure how to respond. "What do you mean? I didn't want him to ask me to the dance," she lied. And she knew Magnus knew she was lying.

"Why do you suddenly like him? Is it because he's 'exotic'? Or different? Or rich? Are you upset from what you heard because you wanted to be figuring those things out or getting settled into a lovely family? Leticia seems to have grown quite fond of you." He stood up quickly, running his hands through his fluffy but perfectly manicured chocolate hair. He shook his head and turned to walk back to the dance.

"Magnus, wait," she called, springing from the curb. She felt the fabric of her dress catch just enough on the rough pavement to give her worry, but not enough to rip the tender layers. "Where is this coming from? Why are you attacking me?" She felt tears threatening to spring forth. Relief came when he stopped. She had never seen the look of anguish on his face that greeted her when he turned around.

"Attacking you? Ivy, I have spent years being there for you, supporting you, holding you, encouraging you, sharing with you, creating memories with you. I have spent years showing you what I have to offer, and give, and falling in love with you for you. And suddenly, this guy sweeps in. You insult him and hit a point of rock bottom I've never seen before, you're suddenly best friends and dreaming of spending nights like tonight with him. Nights that should be our nights, Ivy."

She was stunned. Of all the answers he could have shouted under the buzzing fluorescent streetlight, this was not what she would have expected. "Me? What are you talking about Magnus?"

"How else can I say it? I wanted to ask you tonight. I want to ask you every night. I want you to see me how I see you."

"Oh my God, Mag. I never thought about us like that. I thought you were gay! You never talk about other girls, flirted with other girls, or even made comments about girls in the movies. They'd be prancing around in bikinis, or flopping their perfectly shaped boobs around, and you'd never say anything. I didn't think you liked girls, not that it matters."

"Ivy, I'm not gay. Well, not exclusively. I think a lot of people are beautiful, but I've only felt like I loved you," he replied, downtrodden but animated.

"I…I don't know what to say. I love you, Mag. You're my best friend, and I'll love you no matter what. I just wasn't expecting this. At all," she stammered, shaking her head and trying to find the correct plan of action so she didn't lose her best friend tonight, too.

He took a step forward, reaching out to run his hand over her cheek. "It's now or never," he whispered, pulling her into him and meeting her lips with his.

Their lips touched, and Magnus braced himself. Ivy went as limp as a bag of flour. Her lips turned to Jell-O, plump and bouncy but tight and unforgiving. She pulled away, eyeing Magnus with curiosity, not the sudden burning desire he had initially hoped for. "Um, okay. Well, that was interesting."

"That's not how I envisioned this, and trust me, I've been thinking about this for years. I always thought that would go much, much different," he whispered.

"Maybe it was nerves...should we try again?" she offered, not waiting for him to answer. Spontaneity took over. She wanted to catch him off guard, to take away his ability to over think. Maybe they were soul mates. Taking a step closer until her toes were touching his and they were chest to chest, she wound her long fingers around his neck, pulled him into her, and once again lightly grazed his lips with hers.

"That's awful," Magnus softly replied. "I'm sorry, Ivy, but that's just awful. This may be the worst kiss I've ever had in my life."

They broke out laughing at the absurdity of the situation.

"What did you imagine? Fireworks, butterflies, me falling madly in love with you and being caught off guard that my hero has been in front of me the whole time?"

"Oh don't be stupid, Ivy. Well yes. Yes, I did. But no one will ever be your hero except yourself. You're too hard-headed." He laughed, covering his eyes. "That's exactly what I thought. But I never want to kiss you again."

"Please, don't," she laughed. "I love you, Mag. I always will. And I know you love me. This is never going to change. Ever."

"Promise? I really can't live without you. You're my rock. But now I know that for sure I don't want to live with you."

"Promise," she laughed, holding her stomach as intense

cramping took over from their hysterics.

"Alright. Well, why don't we head home? I need to spend a few hours tonight tearing up a stack of notebooks with your name in little hearts."

CHAPTER TWELVE

*T*he days after the dance seemed to painfully crawl by during class, and then speed up once the final bell rang. Ivy felt the universe had created a time warp, to keep her at school and within arms' reach of Alex. She did her best to avoid him, feigning a sick stomach in Chemistry so that mumbles and one syllable moans were accepted as conversation. She walked different halls between class and lied that her cheap phone had finally died.

When she looked at him, her heart hurt from knowing the girl putting a smile on his face was the girl winning money off of his physique and other bets. She felt parts of her faith crack knowing people saw him for what his family could offer.. Ivy knew him as intelligent, inquisitive, funny at the right unexpected times, and an extremely reliable friend, even after a rough start. Those girls knew him as the son of a famous doctor with a bank account large enough to secure a few future generations.

There were a few days where she was tempted to actually go to her locker, claim her space, and let the Super Six know she was in the bathroom that night. She wanted to look them in the eyes and let them know she knew about their bets, and she had every plan to be a thorn in their side. She imagined their eyes shooting open, their mouths dropping to the floor, and them falling to their knees. They would plead with her to not tell, crying, "We'll do anything!" Of course, she knew that would never happen. With her luck, they'd punch her in the face, break her nose, and she'd get blamed for pushing them over the edge. This was a one-way street, and her only option was to remain silent, even if it ate her alive.

"Mr. Green," she shouted, raising her hand. Alex dropped his beaker at the sudden outburst, the glass breaking into thin slivers and spilling a liquid that promptly began bubbling on the tiles.

"No one move," he replied, his voice booming through the room. "No one move. Did anyone get any liquid on them? Alex, what was in that beaker?"

"That was just blue water."

"No sodium hydroxide?"

"No, Sir. Wait. That wasn't the water..."

"Okay. I'm going to ask everyone to step back and let me clean this up. Ivy, what was so pressing that you had to scare the entire room?"

"I need to go to Mrs. Guinea's office. Now."

"Do you have an appointment?" he asked, not expecting a student from this class to adamantly request a trip to the guidance counselor.

"I don't, and I'm sorry, but I don't care. I need to see her."

"Fine, go. If she has questions, tell her to call down here. I don't have the time to write a hall pass right now." He sighed, agitated.

"Thank you." She grabbed her books, tossed them into her backpack, and avoided eye contact as well as Alex's staccato attempts to get her attention. Bursting through the lab room door, she found herself willfully sprinting down the hallway, hands overflowing with notebooks, pencils, and textbooks. She hadn't run for years, but to her surprise, her body didn't seem to mind. She passed the hall monitor without a second glance, ignored their yelling after her, passed the Principal's office, and didn't stop until she was planted firmly in front of her guidance counselor's door and pounding with her fists.

"Ivy," Mrs. Guinea said, shocked, when she pulled the door open, YouTube videos of mischievous cats played full sound on her computer screen and ripped Twix wrappers cluttering her desktop. "Forgive the mess. It's this baby. I always thought women were full of shit, I mean, lying, when they talked about pregnancy and all the things it does to you. I can't quit eating candy bars and crying over cats being jerks. Ridiculous. Take a seat, take a seat."

Plopping down on the firm faux leather, she suddenly felt out of her depth. She wasn't sure why she felt the urge to come here or talk to a woman she'd rarely heard say three words to over the course of her high school career so far, but she trusted her instinct. And, since her instinct had pointed her here, she trusted that this must be where and how she would find her answers. Maybe she'd find peace of mind. If she didn't, this sophomore year was going to officially drive her to the edge of madness.

"What's the purpose for your visit today," Mrs. Guinea asked, searching through the computer records. "Looks like you're doing really well this year, Ivy. The teachers all left great feedback for you at midterms. Wow, I am so proud of you! Straight A's so far and even a recommendation for placement in a targeted literature class instead of remedial English next year. Teacher says you have unique opinions and are able to derive complex plots from the reading, engaging the other students into serious conversations."

"She did? Huh. I just brought up some points about how Shakespeare was boring and sexist..."

"Do you want to discuss switching classes, or is there a problem we don't know about?" she asked, her voice slowly waning.

"There's a problem. Well, a situation. I mean, I have

this friend, and he really means a lot to me. We got off to a rocky start, but we talked about things, and now we're terrific friends. And I might even like him, maybe, I don't know. Maybe I'm a slug without the ability to comprehend complex emotions."

"Ivy, you're not a slug, but you do need to have a point."

"Right. What would you do if you overheard something that could hurt someone? Someone you really care about?"

Mrs. Guinea straightened herself, leaning over the desk to accurately assess the situation. "Are you saying someone has been threatened? Or is someone in danger?" she asked, her voice direct and free from the effervescence that had been present only a moment earlier.

"No, not exactly. At homecoming, I sort of snuck into the locker room bathroom because I knew there wouldn't be a line. My feet were killing me, so I chilled a little longer than I should have in the haunted handicapped stall. Well, this group of girls came in, and I heard them making…jokes. And talking about a bet they had made involving sexual favors."

"Were these girls being forced into these sexual favors? Is that where you're going with this?" she asked, her concentration laser-focused on the bumbling student in front of her.

"No, no. The sexual favors were with my friend, or they were betting on my friend. And then they were talking about how they needed him because he was rich, and I can't remember everything now. But I feel like I need to tell my friend, and I'm also afraid that if I tell, he's going to get really upset with me and I'll lose him. I'm not sure what's going on this year. I can't quit crying, everything is emotional, and no matter how hard I try, I can't stop caring about other people," she said, her lip starting to quiver.

"I see. You overheard your peers, one of which is involved with a friend of yours, and the things you heard them saying weren't very nice."

"Right. It doesn't sound so bad when you put it like that," Ivy replied.

"Well, this is your friend. Someone you care about, and you know they would be impacted by what you heard. This may even ruin a new relationship for them, and you don't want to be the person who is responsible for that."

"Yes," Ivy nodded in agreement. "That's exactly right. What should I do?"

"That's a very loaded question. You have a few avenues to think about. One road would be to tell them and risk your friendship, depending on which relationship they value the most. Another would be to tell them and then have to carry the emotional burden of the potential fall out of their other relationships. Another would be to not say anything at all and carry that with you, which would likely interfere with your relationship due to feelings of guilt. Since you came to me, I can tell this relationship is extremely important to you. Do you believe your relationship will be able to overcome your honesty?"

"I think so. I'm not sure, but I hope so. My problem is that I don't even know how to start the conversation. I'm not good with talking to people. I usually just clam up. Can you help me?"

"Absolutely. I'm really proud of you for coming to me today. It's a big step to ask for help. Now, let's figure out how to help you move forward with this situation."

Ivy's heart was heavy. The chat with Mrs. Guinea presented a few ways to open the conversation with Alex, and how to handle objections inside of the conversation. While she could never be fully prepared, she did feel confident with the newly acquired tools she would be taking to the table.

The loud double bell indicating the end of the school day rang out, and Ivy burst forth from the bathroom stall she had once again locked herself in. It felt like years since she moved through these halls trying desperately to not be seen, dodging people like a professional football player, twisting and turning like the most skilled ballerina, and delicately making her way through the atrium where if she timed her flight just right, she'd run into Magnus, hop into his car and be escorted home.

She heard her name being shouted behind her, and she knew she had to either walk faster or face a fate worse than death. When she felt the pressure of a hand on her shoulder, she knew her legs didn't quite carry her as fast as she had willed them to move.

"Ivy," Alex called, his voice wrapping over her shoulder – the same one his hand was laying on.

With a little shimmy and outward right turn, she slipped out of his grasp and quickened her pace. She didn't pause, she didn't look back, and she did not acknowledge his presence. She kept her eyes forward with focus as sharp as a surgeon's scalpel. Her breath came in a large gasp when she burst through the atrium doors into the sunlight. The sharp intake of fresh air hit her lungs like a hot poker.

"Ivy, wait up," Alex called out once again.

She heard his feet. His gait was distinct with a slight drag on the right foot, and he always hit harder with his left. Most people wouldn't notice such a subtle characteristic, but for Ivy who spent her life watching and analyzing everyone, the quirk was unique and noteworthy.

"Seriously. Stop," he belted. Her body stopped moving and snapped backward when his hand firmly grasped her upper left arm. "What is going on with you? Talk to me," he said.

His eyes were sincere, and Ivy felt immediate comfort when they met with hers. She stammered, not able to fulfill a complete sentence, and instead, drowning in the guilt of the secret she hid.

"Did someone hurt you?" a soft voice squeaked from his left. Even though she didn't need to look to recognize the voice, her eyes betrayed her and moved on their own accord.

"Oh, no. Not this. Not right now," she stuttered, staring at Leslie's perky face. "No, Alex. You and I need to talk, but not here, and not in front of...of her."

"You are so weird. What's gotten into you?"

The words began in her stomach and filtered up as quickly as bubbles in a freshly popped bottle of champagne. The eruption of words took charge and furiously spilled forth.

"I know all about you, Leslie. At homecoming, I was in the bathroom when you and your bitch squad came in. And I heard it all. All of it," she snarled. "I know about how your friends are only interested in Alex because he's rich, that you guys openly discuss how big his genitals are, and most of all, come to think of it, I'm really curious who won the $325 bet about the actual size of his penis. You did promise them you'd find out by the morning after homecoming. So, who won?"

"I, Ivy," Leslie choked.

"What is she talking about, Leslie?" Alex muttered.

She was stumbling over her words, and Ivy decided enough was enough; this imposter didn't get a chance to try and find the right words. Now, it was if someone grabbed the half-empty bottle of champagne, but kept their thumb over the top, and gave it a good shake. "Alex, don't be stupid. She doesn't care about you. She's using you because you're the new toy at school. You're rich, and they have a bet over when she's going to have sex with you, if she'll be able to handle your, well, penis, and how big it is!" she yelled, forgetting]they were standing just outside the atrium doors where every single student was filing out of the building on their way home. Curious eyes snapped their way, trying to figure out the conversation and why the weird girl who never spoke to anyone was yelling about male genitalia.

"Is that true?" he asked Leslie, dropping her hand.

"No, Alex, of course not. I would never....I didn't.... Why am I even doing this?" she screeched. "No. Absolutely not. This is not true."

Electrified silence hung in the air, sizzling and snapping between the girls. Ivy stared at the rabbit who knew she was backed into a trap, but the rabbit knew the trap was loose and she could shimmy out if she just waited a few more moments.

"You know what, Ivy?" Alex cut in. "This is bad. Even for you. I thought we were friends. But, lately, you've been so weird. Ever since I started to find my place in this school, do things that make me happy, you've been a real pain in the ass. I can't believe you would make up a story like that. Why are you so desperate to bring these people down? They're not mean – you're just a standoffish raging bitch to everyone. And you know what? I don't blame them for the way they treat you. You ask for it, and then you complain about getting what you ask for. This is too much. I don't think we can be friends anymore," he barked, his feet firmly planted, eyes locked on hers.

Their concentration wasn't even dented by the arrival of Magnus. He jogged across the courtyard and yelled out some sort of nerdy greeting that referenced one of their favorite 80s movies. It fell on uncaring deaf ears.

"What in the world is going on here?" he asked quizzically. With one look around the faces, he knew. "Oh, no. You didn't. Did you?" She nodded. "Damnit, Ivy. Why here? You weren't supposed to say anything. You PROMISED me you wouldn't say anything!"

"You knew about this, too?" Alex gasped. "Are you part of this, Magnus? Great. Just great."

"Can we just leave, Baby?" Leslie cooed. "Come on, I want to get out of here."

They turned to walk away. Alex and Ivy stubbornly held their locked gaze until the very last second. Ivy sighed and stamped her foot.

"You'll see, Alex," she yelled. "She is lying to you. She's not your friend!"

"Enough, Ivy," Magnus hissed. "Start walking. Right now. Get your ass in my car."

CHAPTER THIRTEEN

"*I* can't believe you! We agreed that we weren't going to say anything, and he had to find out on his own," Magnus yelled. He threw open Ivy's front door and ushered her inside like a child.

The car ride home from school had been silent and tense; Ivy stared out the window, huffing, rolling her eyes and doing her best to deflect the onslaught of typical, "What were you thinking?" style questions. Truthfully, she hadn't been thinking, and why anyone would question if she WAS thinking was beyond her. Even though she spent a lot of time watching other people and analytically assessing their actions, she spent very little time examining the root of her own actions.

"Alex deserved to know," she shouted back, throwing her treasured black leather backpack to the floor, not even cringing as it skidded over the threadbare carpet. "That bitch had the nerve to look me in the eye, call me a liar and act like what I was saying was the most far-fetched thing she'd ever heard."

"And that is exactly what we knew would happen, Ivy," Magnus exclaimed, his hands as animated as his face, both furiously telling stories of their own. "I know it feels like the right thing to do, but we agreed we weren't going to be the ones to step in."

Ivy huffed, anger seething through her body and for the first time in her life, she understood what it meant to be seeing red. A soft pop erupted behind her left temple, releasing a wave of pain over her forehead. The room began to tilt and list, colors slid over her vision, and her knees weakened. "He needed to know," she whispered, grabbing her head and crumbling to her knees with a dull thud.

Terrified by the sudden change in Ivy, Magnus threw his bag, jumping to her side just in time to catch her shaking body before she collapsed.

"Ivy...Ivy... Talk to me. Take a deep breath. Focus on my voice, and try to answer my questions," he calmly whispered, cradling her head and lightly stroking her cheeks. He recognized the signs of a panic attack immediately, having had his share the last few years. He could see the dilation of her pupils, her pulse quickening in the veins of her neck, throbbing with strong intensity and visibly vibrating under her skin. "What's your favorite color?" he asked, slowly and gently rocking his friend as she gasped, trying to figure out what was happening.

"Black, like my soul," she choked.

"Good, good. Your brain still works," he softly chuckled. "What's your favorite band?"

"What genre and what year?" she replied.

"Your favorite car?"

"1968 Corvette Stingray, cherry red glossy paint, not metallic, no racing stripes, chrome accents, white quilted leather."

"Beautiful, car," he cooed, softening his rocking as her breathing steadied. "Your favorite food?"

"Pizza, but only from Pizza King with the small pepperoni bits and the bbq sauce, dipped in that delicious French dressing," she sighed. "Oh my goodness, I am so hungry."

Magnus laughed a deep hearty chuckle, no longer afraid of pushing her panic attack over the edge of uncharted territory. "You're going to be just fine, Ivy. Was that your first panic attack?"

"Is that what that was? Yes. My heart is pounding," she said, placing her fingertips upon the thick vein bobbing on her wrist, feeling the thumps push against her pads simultaneously with the heavy pounds she felt slowly calming in her chest.

"It's going to go away. Just stay here for a moment and keep chatting with me. We'll get you some Tylenol for your head. I'm going to assume you don't have any juice. Once you're good, I'll scoot home and get some juice and snacks real quick."

"Mom's been really good about making sure I can stay alive," she chuckled. "Ever since Dad's birthday, it's like we have a new start. I mean, it's still rough at times, but we're both trying. That's all we can do...try. I haven't missed a single breakfast in the last month, and she keeps some sort of liquid that claims to be juice even though it's highly processed corn syrup and artificially flavored liquid."

"Now I really know you're going to be okay," Magnus replied. He gently pushed her shaking fingers from her wrist, taking over to monitor the slowing of her heart rate. "Well, some of the over processed faux juice may be what you need right now. A little glucose does the body good when it's been through a shock." He gently prodded her to sit up, and then helped her slide to her feet, his arm securely wrapped around her waist as they muddled towards the kitchen. "You have Tylenol in the bathroom? You'll probably want to take two. It'll help with the headache, and your body might hurt from all of your muscles tightening."

"Yeah, second shelf. I think I'm going to make a pizza. Any preference, Mag? Pepperoni or sausage?" She turned around, but he was already down the hall, heading for the bathroom. Magnus was a fantastic guy, a fantastic friend, someone who meant the world to her life. If only that kiss after the dance hadn't been so damn bad.

The front door creaked open, and two pairs of feet stomped in, pulling Ivy and Magnus' attention away from their over-cooked and slightly freezer burnt pizza dinner.

Crust crumbles slipped from the corners of Ivy's mouth as she called out a confused greeting towards the front door, just beyond her field of vision. Her body tightened when she heard the response, eyes frozen in fear, the memories of helplessness and confusion from the panic attack that took over her body only a few moments before flooding through her mind.

"Hey..." Alex answered.

"I found this handsome young brown kid out front, Ivy. This must be the boy you've been talking about. Your lab partner? I wasn't sure at first. It's not every day you come home to find a strange dark-skinned person on your steps. Wasn't sure if he was here to mow the grass or rob us, but it turns out, he's here to chat with you." She laughed, her seemingly innocent chuckles carrying around the thin corner until they rested firmly on the slice of pizza in Ivy's hand, tainting the once delicious treat with the inedible flavor of trepidation.

"Alex?" she asked. "What...what are you doing here?"

Magnus pushed his hand against her forearm, gently telling her to stay seated, stay breathing, and stay present. Giving her arm a slight squeeze, he brought her eyes to meet his. "Something happened, or he wouldn't be here. Let's find out what it is."

"Okay," she whispered, closing her eyes and filling her body with a deep breath that occupied every inch from her nostrils to the tiny sacs that inflated in her lungs.

"Ooh, Pizza. Do you mind?" her mom asked, sliding into an open chair around the large round table and pulling a slice of pizza from the tray in one swift movement. "Mm. A little burnt, oven and freezer, but not too bad for clearance special, ay?" she asked, quirking her brows with a smile and tapping Ivy on the shoulder. With a laugh she looked at the deepened shades along the overly crispy crust and turned to Alex. "Look," she said, holding the thin crust up against his skin like a painter taking the measurements of a subject with his thumb. "The crust matches you! It's a multicultural pizza."

Ivy gasped. She wanted to be shocked at the casual ignorance her mother was displaying, but the last few months came full circle. She blamed her initial ignorance on not knowing any black people, and from jokes that circulated around school. Watching the ease at which her mother spat out what she thought were funny jokes, she found her mind scanning all of the repressed memories of inappropriate conversations. There was the time she called a Mexican baby at a church baptism 'bean dip', the Chinese child at the buffet Ching-Ching or zipper boy, and all of the times they would be driving through the city, hitting the lock button on the doors as soon as anyone pulled up next to them who wasn't white. They could pull up in a $100,000 Mercedes G-Wagon and her mother would quickly lock the doors, pitch out her cigarette, and roll up the window.

She shook her head, stumbling over what words she was looking for and what she needed to say, finally finding the courage to look Alex in the face. Her mouth hung open, she had no words for him or her mother.

"It's okay, Ivy," he whispered. His face told her it wasn't okay. His face told her that even though he was used to being in situations like this, he never got used to them and every time they dug away at his soul little by little. When he shifted his eyes back to the floor, a look of shame came into place, and he bit his lip.

Eagerly working through her second piece of pizza, smacking her lips greedily as little dribbles of oil from the cheap overly processed cheese dribbled from the corners of her mouth, Ivy's mother sat firm, oblivious to the shifting tension and unease circling her.

"Mother," Ivy coughed, thumbing her fingers on the table. She wasn't sure if this was the right time to try and educate her, or if that would embarrass Alex more, or cause her to say something even more unacceptable, or if she would even be able to do an adequate job at bringing her attention to why the entire conversation she had just laughed her way through was grossly unacceptable. And, given the way today had gone, Ivy wasn't sure she could control her emotions and not dive deep into the archives of racist jokes, inappropriate statements in public, and the way she unknowingly treated people around her, teaching those around her that it was okay to treat other humans in that manner.

The more Ivy thought about all of the situations, the madder she became that they happened in public areas, overheard by other people, and no one said anything. She wondered what would have happened if one person had spoken up. Would she have had her own eyes opened through the words of someone else? Would she have fought that person for being too nosy, or too sensitive, or too boring without a sense of humor? Would she have brushed them off or would she have listened?

"What?" Ivy's mom returned sarcastically, waiting for the rest of the sentence that was hanging unspoken in the air while her daughter frantically waded through a muddy pit of memories pulling her down like quicksand.

Magnus squeezed her arm and nodded towards Alex. Alex slightly shook his head, not strong enough to be caught in her mother's peripheral vision but enough to let Ivy know this wasn't a bridge to cross right now.

"We have a lot to talk about. Do you care if we go to my room? Or would you go to your room and not be a nosy beast?" she asked through gritted teeth.

"Gotcha. Mom isn't welcome at the teenager party.

Carry on, carry on. Next time you stop by," she said, looking at Alex, "just ring the doorbell so you don't scare us or get introduced to a neighbor's .38."

"Holy shit," Ivy whispered under her breath, loud enough for her words to not go unnoticed.

"Lighten up, it's just a joke," she replied, patting Ivy on the back while she pushed herself to her feet, the chair screeching over the linoleum floor that threatened to pull back against the decade's old glue that somehow still held the tiles to the baseboards.

Ivy apologized profusely to Alex, head in her hands. She found herself arriving at a mythical part of life, a part that people believe only happens to other unfortunate souls and never to them, when they realize influences, good or bad, have had the opportunity to shape who they are. And, there's a time in everyone's life where they have the opportunity to decide if they are stronger than previous influences.

"Welcome to my house," she quietly said, suddenly aware of what that meant. Her house, her trailer, on the outskirts of the district, where people of Alex's standing didn't visit. Her house that could fit into his garage, where everything inside would have a combined value of less than his backyard. Her house, where the carpet exhibited signs of male patterned baldness, the television was trying to channel aliens through its antennae with foil tips, and the color scheme hadn't changed in twenty years. "Do you want a drink? We have, um, water, green tea, and this stuff that's supposed to be juice but it's more like a science experiment."

Politely declining, he cut through the awkwardness and swiftly moved to the purpose for his visit. After the blow up outside of school, he left to take Leslie home. Something didn't feel right, and he continued to question her when she came clean. She not only admitted to the conversation in the bathroom but also admitted to the bet.

"But she says she was just going along with everything to keep them happy. Pressure to fit in she said..." he paused, breaking eye contact. "I know this sounds ridiculous, and believe me, I'm not happy about this."

"Do you believe her?" Ivy asked, her voice calm and steady without a hint of judgment. "You know her better than we do, Alex. I've only talked to her in the locker bay. I heard that conversation in the bathroom, and it really bothered me."

"That's why I'm here," Alex quietly replied. "I'm sorry that I didn't believe you. And, I'm sorry for what I said. You are my friend. Both of you. It occurred to me once I got here that if her friends were talking like that, they probably had those conversations with their boyfriends, my teammates."

"You had every right to not believe me, Alex. It would make sense that I might try to sabotage them. I know. Truthfully, Leslie was really nice to me after the science fair. I actually liked her, even though she called me out for being rude, too." She gave a small laugh of recognition and then continued. "Do you think maybe it was just the other girls? Just because she was in the room doesn't mean she's guilty, you know?"

"I know. I thought about that on the drive over. I need to know more about what you heard – but just the truth. No excess embellishment or emotion, okay?"

"Okay," she agreed. She recounted homecoming the best she could remember, what she heard, whose voice she thought the statements belonged to. "Is it as bad as I thought it was?" she asked, doubting everything.

"Well, it doesn't make me happy. I can't say it's any worse than conversations I've had, but I've never made a bet about another person. But I know plenty of boys who have."

Magnus cleared his throat, sitting up and leaning into the table. "If I can interrupt, I don't think your teammates have anything to do with this, either.. They'd just try to win the bet by taking first look, you are in a locker room after all," he paused, shaking his head with a chuckle "The other way to look at this is if the boys knew their girls had a bet about you, I don't think they'd like you very much."

"Another valid point," Alex replied.

"What happened with you and Leslie?" Ivy cut in, trying to figure out if telling Alex was still the right thing to do or if this was an important lesson on how to control her emotions, judge situations, and learn what needs to be discussed and what didn't. "I don't hate her. Maybe I'm jealous of her."

"Maybe?" Magnus scoffed. "Definitely. But I'm not sure that matters right now. I don't think they consider you and Alex to be friends, or are even concerned about you in the big picture. If this situation were a Venn diagram, we wouldn't even be in the center. We'd be some far outlying circle that no one understood why it was even drawn on the paper."

"What do you think I should do?" Alex asked, looking his friends over, his eyes begging for advice.

Ivy was caught off-guard. She had asked Magnus for advice, Magnus had given her advice, but this was the first time she might impact someone else's future, or give advice that might help or hurt a few relationships. The burden was heavy, and she wasn't going to take the responsibility lightly. The time for making careless observations was finished.

"I'm not sure, Alex. I don't think I can answer that for you, and I don't think I should answer that for you. I'm not sure what I'd do. I do know that if I cared about someone, and if I felt like I knew them, I'd look at the situation from all angles. Over ice cream...with chocolate sauce...maybe some gummy bears..."

Alex paused. "Gummy bears? She does love gummies. Hey, Ivy?"

"Yeah," she whispered.

"Do you think your mom should have tea with my mom?"

Ivy laughed. "Are you nuts? I don't want your mom to end up in jail. I really like her. I'll talk to her, Alex. I promise. I just need to figure out how. Any advice for me?"

"Honestly? No. You know her better. You've listened. You've learned. Why? How did someone get to you?"

She sighed. "I don't know, Alex. It's scary."

Alex nodded his head in agreement. "Welcome to my life."

CHAPTER FOURTEEN

"*T*oday is just crawling along, isn't it?" Ivy groaned, swinging her leg over the cafeteria table's attached bench. "I really wish they'd get us chairs. These benches are too low and not close enough to properly eat. It's a wonder I leave lunch with clean clothes every day."

"Wow, you are in a mood today! What crawled up your ass, laid its eggs and is now eating you from the inside out?"

Eww, gross Mag. That's the most repulsive thing I've ever heard. But, before you can say anything else that might even be worse than that, it's just school, man. It's just school. These stupid papers are so pointless – I'm in classes with kids complaining about writing a five-page report on a book I could have read in grade school. They act like it's rocket science to complete basic assignments. And, don't get me started on American History. We had a test this week. Sean Jackson was arguing with my teacher over whether or not the Constitution was actually written in 1787. And, when he couldn't talk his way out of getting that answer wrong, he started arguing over the stupidest answers on the test. He even argued some other stupid question on Philadelphia. Magnus, I have no hope in the world if these are the kids who might run our country someday. What in the hell are we going to do?"

"Why don't you run? If you're so terrified of your peers one day coming to power, why don't you start your own path to political glory?"

"Gross, Mag. Again. Gross. You know politics is not my thing. I'm not sure what my thing is, yet, but I know it's not politics."

"And you're worried that politics will suddenly be their thing? Please. They're not going to run anything except the dishwasher at a diner. They're hopeless."

Ivy paused, understanding the analogy, but painfully aware Magnus had not yet realized he just insulted her mother. These slight remarks happened relatively often, and they always sat with her the wrong way. For someone who confessed his undying love and inability to live without her, he seemed to forget where she came from when he quietly slipped back into status quo mode. She watched him shoveling forkfuls of instant mashed potatoes and corn that was sweeter than any natural farm grown corn should be into his mouth.

"Are you not hungry? If you're not going to eat, can I have your roll?" he asked, eyeing the fluffy buttermilk yeast roll greedily.

She huffed, looked him in the eyes, split open the roll, and shoved half into her mouth without breaking contact. The soft pillowy cloud turned into a ball of deliciously sweet dough immediately in her mouth, and she slowly slumped, feeling relief settle in.

"You weren't hungry. You were hangry. Damn, girl. I'm impressed. You might have a future in speed eating. Have you heard of that? There are guys in New York City and Japan, and they can eat a boatload of hotdogs. Just bam, bam, bam," he said, imitating someone throwing hot dogs into their mouth.

"That's disgusting, and exhilarating all at once. Do they make money?"

"I think so. I'm sure they get prize money, or sponsorship, or something. I mean, it's 2018, and we're in the digital age. You can get paid and make money for doing anything, as long as you do it well. Isn't technology great?"

Ivy would have answered yes. She would have embraced his flowing speech of the wonders of how quickly society has grown in terms of technological advances. She would have fawned over her favorite app and how it changed her life or some of the neat products she'd read about in magazines during study hall. But she never got the chance.

In a blur of words, sounds, temperatures, and textures, Ivy became the center of lunch break attention. She felt every set of eyes in the lunch room snap to her at the same time she thought she heard someone call her a bitch; at the same time a warm sticky liquid landed on her scalp and began its speedy journey down the strands of her hair, the bridge of her nose, her neck, her décolletage, and torso until her lap became flooded with the soup of the day and her ears became inundated with the curse words of angry girls.

"It's the Super Six," Magnus whispered, frozen in place.

In a perfect world, she would have jumped up and thrown a punch at her assaulter, or dumped her drink over one of their heads, or picked up her chicken sandwich that was loaded down with ketchup and mustard and pull a Gordon Ramsey. She'd smash the sloppy condiment loaded buns on the sides of someone's face and scream as loud as she could by tapping into her inner drill sergeant, telling them what an idiot sandwich they were. In a perfect world, she would have had the courage to do something, anything.

But this wasn't a perfect world, and she sat on the bench, stunned. Her mind would think of a hundred reactions, and her body would refuse them all. To her astonishment, for once this tumultuous and testing year, the tears did not threaten to come. There was a chance that even her tears were receding deep into the depths of her private hell, or maybe the bright red broth running down her face tricked her body into thinking she was already crying.

She wasn't sure how long she sat there, unmoving. It

could have been seconds; it might have been minutes. Time seemed to be speeding past her in visual waves of vibrating light, and at the same time, crawling so painfully slow that she could see the most minute micro-expressions on the faces of people around her.

"I don't think you heard me the first time," Jenna Caldwell said, tipping a salad coated in neon orange French dressing over her head to accompany the soup. "You are a bitch."

Ivy's mind raced. Where were the teachers? Where were the room monitors? Was she so inconsequential that having food dumped over her body wasn't seen as a situation worthy of interfering in? Why was Magnus just sitting there?

She felt the cold fizzle of a soda rain down, joined swiftly by another, and another. There was not an inch of dry skin or clothing on the top 3/4s of her body, the soda pooling in the small pouch that stuck out from the back of her slightly ill-fitting jeans.

When the downpour stopped, she gingerly wiped the excess liquid off of her face, smearing a healthy amount of black mascara over her cheeks to intensify the current state of her disastrous appearance. Her eyes snapped towards Magnus, and she found him tightly held in a linebacker bear hug with a dirty sock tightly pulled over his mouth. In the background, subtle sounds of yelling started to flow to her ears, beginning as a methodical womp womp womp and evolving into a string of free-flowing words, insults, and accusations.

Her eyes focused on the crowd that had circled the group like hungry wolves eager for a bite of their leader's kill. They cheered, chanted, tossed scraps of food into the hastily constructed ring of bodies. Turning around to run, she instead found herself face to face with six of the worst people alive.

"Just because you want to give your virginity to Alex

and he won't touch you," one yelled, fading into another screaming, "...you tried to ruin Leslie..." into another shouting, "...trash like you..." and on, and on, and on.

Jenna stepped back up, a piece of cake loaded down with syrupy fruit and whipped cream in her hand. She lifted it, preparing to smash the inedible confection in Ivy's face to finish the assault. "You don't know the first thing about girl code. You should be ashamed. You are a disgrace to females everywhere. To feminism," she shouted, raising the cake in the air, the crowd crying out in agreement.

Ivy wasted no time. She reeled back, remembering what her dad taught her about not tucking her thumb when she balled her fingers into a fist, and put every ounce of pent up aggression, held back frustration, and hope that she had stored in her body and pushed it straight into Jenna's face.

"Ladies, fighting is not acceptable. I am extremely disappointed in all of you," Principal Penny scolded, pacing past the silent girls lined up in his office. "This is an institution for learning, not for immature drama and gossip. Sit down. All of you."

One by one, they fell into the closest wool covered scratchy office chair, no doubt upholstered by the devil himself. Ivy always theorized that these chairs were purposely created to be as uncomfortable as possible to lessen student meetings or intensify punishment.

"Not you," Principal Penny said, gesturing wildly to Ivy. "Not in those clothes. You can stand."

"Principal Penny, can I please go to the nurse and get some backup clothes? Or the lost and found? This is ridiculous," she replied, pulling another piece of lettuce and a sunflower seed from the soda matted strands that hung in clumps around her face.

"Absolutely not. You're not changing a thing until we get to the bottom of this. As far as I'm concerned, every single one of you are in deep trouble. You," he said, pointing squarely to Ivy. "Violence? In my cafeteria? You broke Jenna's nose. She may even need surgery."

"She was getting a nose job anyway," one of the Super Six said, laughing. "This will only make it cheaper for her parents."

"That was self-defense. Jenna just dumped soup, salad, and soda on me, and was about to smash cake in my face. I could have been the one with the broken nose," Ivy exclaimed, shocked that the conversation was turning to putting her on trial. She noticed the other girls were smirking, confident that they would be let off the hook, soaring by on their reputation and need to have a clean record for college applications.

"Oh, yes, Principal Penny. This girl is a monster. I can't believe she hit Jenna like that. And you should have heard the nasty rumors she spread. Poor Leslie, she's practically in hiding now because of this girl."

"That's not true! You were the ones in the bathroom making bets about how big Alex's penis is, how quickly Leslie could have sex with him, and which one of you deserved him the most because his parents are richer than yours and Leslie doesn't need any more money," she yelled so loudly that Principal Penny's secretary leaned over in her desk to peer through the thin sliver of a window and include herself in the conversation as well. "And I didn't start any rumors. The only person I told was Alex, well, and Magnus. Okay, and Mrs. Guinea, but that one was just because I didn't know if I should tell Alex or not."

"You told MRS. GUINEA?" girl number three shrieked. "She does water aerobics with my mother. If she tells my mom, I'm going to be grounded for life! I swear to God, trailer trash girl, if this gets to my mom, what you went through today won't compare to the hell I will rain down on you. You can't touch me, but I can ruin you," she screamed.

Principal Penny slammed his hands on his desk, his

computer shaking and his metal mesh pencil cup caving to the pressure in the room, spilling its collection of ornate fountain pens over the desk and on to the tightly pulled carpet. "Enough! No one will be doing anything else. And, let me promise you something. If one of you thinks they're going to continue this event once you leave this room, I'll be coming for you. And trust me when I say that in this room, I'm the only one who can't be touched."

"Can I talk to Mrs. Guinea?" Ivy whispered. "Please."

Principal Penny sighed and rubbed his hands over his forehead. "Ivy, go to the nurse. Get some other clothes, please. Maybe even go to the gym and shower for God's sake."

"Do I need a pass?"

"No," he yelled, slamming his fists back on the thick oak desk. "Go. Now. The whole damn school knows about this, and I'm sure no one is going to stop you."

Moving quickly, she bent down and scooped up her backpack before fumbling with the door and excusing herself to the freedom of the wide open hallways, free of the confines that felt like a stall leading her to slaughter. Turning the corner, just out of reach of the administrative offices, she shrieked as her body collided heavily against another body, moving quickly through the hallways at a frantic pace. Shoes squealed, books fell to the ground, and the unfortunate student that now shared a bit of the afternoon's excitement from misfortunate contact bounced off of her body, to the wall, and to the floor.

"Oh, shit. I'm so sorry," she forcefully exhaled, furiously scooping up stray papers, trying her best to not drip soup or soda on the stack of loose sheets.

"Ivy," Alex exclaimed. "I heard about what happened. I've been looking for you everywhere. I went by your class, but you weren't there. Are you okay?"

"Yes. No… Yes."

"You don't look okay," he said, hesitating.

"If I don't look okay, then why the hell did you ask? Look at me. I'm covered in soup, soda, and salad. I'm potentially going to be expelled. I'm now even more of a laughing stock than I was before. I am absolutely hopeless, Alex. Just hopeless."

Every ligament in her body faded from sinew to rubber and against her mental will, her physical will gave way. Sliding down the wall that only moments before was holding her into place, she slumped on the floor with a deep sigh. Every ounce of her being was exhausted. She had no tears, no words, no emotions, and no fucks left to give.

"I have an idea," Alex whispered. "Don't ask questions, don't speak, don't argue, and follow any directions that I give you."

"Why?" she sighed.

"I knew you were going to ask that. Follow my instructions, okay? We're going to get out of here. If anyone stops us, cry or something. You've been doing that really well. But, most importantly, don't talk. If you open your mouth, we'll be stuck here. Keep it closed, no matter how hard it is."

CHAPTER FIFTEEN

"*W*here in the world are we going?" Ivy asked. "Please don't tell me this was all a ruse and you're going to take my body out to a cornfield in Shelbyville and dump me."

"Absolutely not. Honestly, that'd be too much work when I could have just turned you over to the rabid beasts in Principal Penny's office. You need a shower, but we can't be seen by either of our parents. I have an idea, just hold tight," he replied, turning up the music to drown out anything she may have countered with.

She shifted her body, slipping on the old quilt Alex draped over his passenger seat before he let her climb in the car. Their exit from the school had been fast and furious. Alex's idea of sneaking out was to speed walk through the most popular halls in the school and avoid eye contact. Ivy would have suggested they take the quieter halls, hide in nooks and crannies, and twist their way through the shadows like cartoon ninjas until they reached the parking lot. His method proved to be the stronger option. The two hall monitors they had run into didn't even question them, likely because every single person in the school knew exactly what had gone down at lunch and Ivy still looked like she had just climbed out of an open grave after a Mardi Gras party.

With the music blasting, the windows open, and the cool mid-afternoon spring air creeping in to the car, the afternoon would have been one for the books had it not immediately followed an afternoon that deserved to be locked away, placed into wet cement, wrapped with chains and weights, and dumped into the deepest lake within a one day's drive. The winding country roads played a game of hide and seek with the cornfields, currently barren, brown and showing the secrets they hid for six months each year.

"Here we go," Alex said, pulling in to the parking lot next to a colorful playground. Noticing the look of confusion Ivy was shooting his way, he continued to explain. "They have a splash pad. You're going to go run through it, try to not mow down any kids, and wash that nasty mix off. Then, you're going to go to the bathrooms right over there," he explained, turning around to dig in an oversized Nike bag in his back seat, "and put on these. Don't worry, they're clean." He handed her his practice game tracksuit and a black t-shirt. "They're not the most stylish, but this should work. Oh, and hold out your hand," he commanded, laughing as he squirted a palm full of heavily scented body gel into her open hand.

"I'm going to look so weird sudsing myself up in a baby splash park," she laughed. "I swear, this is the year of firsts. I hope life doesn't take this as a cue for what to test me with year after year."

"You're going to look a lot weirder if you don't make an attempt to clean yourself up. And you're going to feel a lot worse if you make me take you home where we might run into your mom and have to explain what all this is."

"Oh, Alex. About my mom..." she started. "The other day..."

"It's okay."

"No, Alex. It's not. I just don't know what to say. I don't know if I will know what to say. I can say that I'm sorry, but I know that won't be enough."

"Ivy, if you drip soap in my car, on top of all of that other junk sitting on you right now, I'm going to kick your ass.

Lunch won't be your only fight for the day. Please, go. We can talk about this later, okay?"

"Okay. Um, I'll be right back. I'm going to go shower in a kiddie pool...in public," she laughed. "Whatever you do, please do not take a photo, video, or put this anywhere on social media. This is between you and me, a story that we'll tell down the road at graduation or a high school reunion. Okay?"

"If you insist. But I'm sure if we turned this into a vlog, you would get some serious ad revenue," he joked before pushing her gently as a signal that he wasn't going to tell her to leave the car again.

She used her soap-free hand to free her sticky body from the luxurious car, unable to control the gag that escaped when a burst of wind circled her body, pushing the sour scent of her many layers firmly up her nostrils. The smell was overwhelming, and she eagerly slapped the soapy gel into her hair, working the concentrated liquid through her sticky and clumped strands with each step closer to the collection of brightly colored mushroom shapes that would soon wash her sins of the day from her body.

The chilly water cascaded over her head and shocked her senses, instantly bringing an eruption of bubbles, the soap working as furiously as her fingers to scrub her body clean. She knew the three mothers who were at the swings, but wouldn't dare allow their kids in the water for fear of them coming down with pneumonia, were staring at her like an unknown parasite had just infiltrated their safe zone. In her peripheral vision, she saw one mother grab her kids and begin to usher them towards the car.

Feeling slightly refreshed but still sticky, she motioned to Alex. Miming 'I need more soap,' by acting like she was washing her body, but there weren't any bubbles, or smacking an empty soap bottle, she set the next steps of her devious plan in place. Sure, a little more soap wouldn't hurt, but having someone to jump the frustration out with in the water would definitely help.

A smile grew over her face when Alex got the hint, stepping out of his black BMW and walking towards her with the body wash.

That was enough soap to wash an elephant, Ivy.

"Hey, Alex, do you have another set of clothes in your car? I was just thinking, what if I don't like the tracksuit?"

He hesitated, scowling at the absurdity of her question. "If I were you, I'd just be happy to not smell like a dump truck, but sure. Yeah, I have some shorts and another t-shirt," he replied, stepping forward to give her another healthy squeeze of soap.

Taking full advantage of the opportunity, Ivy relied on the element of surprise, grabbed his forearm, and pulled until his body shot forward into the mushroom waterfall.

"What the hell," he screeched. "Oh my God, it's so cold. Why is it so cold?"

"Jump around," Ivy commanded, bobbing around him while channeling her inner boxer. "You'll warm up." She swiftly dobbed a healthy glob of shower gel on top of his head. "Now you're stuck with me, lalalalala," she laughed, continuing to bounce around him, letting joy overtake her. She watched her frustrations slip down the massive grated floor drain along with the thousands of bubbles they were creating that the pipe probably wasn't prepared for.

"Well, I can see you're pretty proud of yourself. But at least you're smiling and happy, that's good for you. Maybe not so good for me," Alex replied, his outlook also lifting and his willingness to entertain the charade increasing. He cupped his hands on the edge of the flowing water until the crevice was full, quickly throwing the collected liquid in Ivy's face. "Waterbomb," he screamed before running away.

"Oh no you didn't," she squealed, trying to do the same but too impatient to master the method. She resigned her plan of attack to kicking puddles and trying her best to splash her friend.

"What's going on here? Out of the water, now," a loud voice boomed. "Do you two have ID?"

The teens shot around to face a uniformed policeman, hands on his hip, looking none too happy about an unruly disturbance.

This is a park for children. We've had a call about you two disturbing the peace and lewd acts in public," he said, sternly.

Ivy peered over his shoulder to see a perfectly manicured mother in black cigarette pants, ballet flats with a big gold logo buckle, and a perfectly pressed polka dotted blouse tucked in halfway staring at them with a smirk and crossed arms. When their eyes met, she tweaked her head, the silent language of, "Haha, I win. Gotcha!"

"Sorry, officer. We'll go," Ivy replied, giving her hair one last wet shake to make sure she had all the suds out. She stepped forward and bent down to pick up her socks, moving towards her shoes. "We didn't mean any harm."

"Not so fast," he called. "ID's, both of you."

"But –"

"Just do what he says," Alex replied, hushing Ivy and pushing her forward. "We need to go to my car. It's that one over there," he said, pointing towards the expensive black BMW.

The lanky officer followed the duo towards the car, eager to get his hands on their IDs, which he quickly grabbed as soon as they were offered. Excusing himself to scan their licenses and call in the resolution of the disturbance, he turned back to his squad car and confidently walked away.

"This is so stupid. We weren't doing anything wrong, that mom over there just has a stick up her perfect little butt," Ivy huffed. "And you, why did you tell me to be quiet? We could have walked away if you would have let me talk."

"No, Ivy, we couldn't have. That's not how it works."

"In what world? Have you ever met a cop before? Bat your eyes, apologize, and get on with your life after promising to behave," she said, gesticulating with her hands, rolling them in the air, leaning forward towards him and inadvertently occupying his bubble of personal space.

"In what world? In my world, Ivy. In my world. I am a black man in a white neighborhood. I don't get to bat my eyes and beg for forgiveness. I get to shut up, stay quiet, do what he asks, and hope I walk away without being arrested or killed. That's my world, Ivy," he growled, shaking his head, frustration escaping into the air around them.

Every fiber of her being wanted to fight back. Her mind swirled for what words she could throw back to stand her ground. She wanted to be angry at him for giving up so easily, or for pushing her to be submissive in the face of something she felt wasn't that big of a deal. Her tongue would flick in anticipation of finally finding the words to speak, but they would never make it out. Whatever words she thought she found stayed tightly locked inside her vocal cords.

"Alright, you two. You look like good kids, I think, anyway. I'm going to let you go with a warning. This is a kid's park. If you want to play here, start babysitting or bring your kid sister if you have one. If you don't, I don't want to see you back here. I'm going to ask you to get back in your car and leave," the officer said, his green eyes shining in the sun, full of judgment and superiority.

"Thank you, Officer," Alex quietly replied, gently taking his driver's license and heading to the car.

Officer, can we go to the bathroom first? I'd really appreciate the chance to change before I get sick from our foolishness," Ivy purred, shrugging coyly with a smirk. She felt Alex's eyes burning into the side of her head.

"Quickly. I'm going to sit here for five minutes. If you're not gone by the time my phone's alarm goes off, you'll get a ticket for loitering and disturbing the peace. Deal?"

"Deal," she squealed, grabbing the dry clothes from the front seat of Alex's car and turning towards the small cinder block pool house. She reached the heavy metal door and turned around to see Alex hadn't followed. He was still standing by the car, his hands tightly clasped in front of him, head and eyes down to the ground, water dripping from his frame into a soft puddle around his bare feet.

The music stayed soft, barely audible over the incoming bursts of fresh country air. The black BMW drifted down the oil and gravel paved roads, small flecks of rock gently tickling the underbelly of the car; the sun turning in to itself, fading from brilliant yellow to a soft orange and beginning to paint the sky with pinks and lavenders on its journey to sleep.

"That happens to you a lot?" Ivy said, finally breaking the silence.

"You mean I just show up places and scare people? Have the cops called on me for being a young kid? Worry about driving just a little too fast, a little too slow, or turning down the wrong street? Yeah. All the time."

Ivy paused. Deep down, she knew he'd say yes even though she hoped he'd say no, what just happened was a fluke. But to hear him confirm her fears was unsettling. In her mind, deep in her private thoughts, she had already justified the water park incident. They were loud, they were making what might be considered a mess, and they were overage. Even though she was able to brush off what happened, she also knew that if she were doing the same foolishness with Magnus, or a girl, they would have gotten dirty looks, but no one would have called the cops.

The car slowed down, gravel popping under the tires as it came to rest on the shoulder just off an access road into a cornfield. Alex collected a handful of dry clothes from the backseat and stepped outside, never saying another word about Ivy's question. She could feel the heaviness in his breath, the frustration and sadness that lingered between the two of them. In this small cubicle, they were both sixteen-year-old sophomores at one of the best schools in the state. They were both fun-loving, slightly irresponsible at times teenagers who wanted to enjoy life. They were both good kids who genuinely enjoyed other people and thought the best of everyone they met. But Ivy just had the truth handed to her on a silver platter, and she was having a challenge digesting her bites.

Alex slung off his wet clothes, letting them smack to the ground in a sloppy heap that would soon turn in to a sandy, grainy mess. His muscles reflected the last waning rays of the sun, beams of fading light settling perfectly into the crevices of his sculpted and athletic body. With his clothes on, he looked slim and healthy. With the layers peeled off, his physique was impeccable, and Ivy gasped. She had only seen carved bodies in the movies and suddenly felt an urge to start attending more games if she was able to sneak peeks at these perfect bodies.

"Hey, Alex," she called out the window. "You didn't tell me you were hiding bricks under your shirt." She smiled when a chuckle slipped from his shaking head.

"You're stupid. Real stupid," he replied. His shoulders relaxed a little, but the tenseness still sat in his neck, and probably would until he could find the inner strength to forgive the policeman for just doing his job and the park mom for being ignorant and judgemental.

Bending over to pick up his soaking wet clothes, Ivy saw him cringe when his hands felt the layer of grit that had quickly settled into the damp threads. He would have no choice except to dump the pile into the trunk, where they landed with a heavy thunk, spreading gravel, sand, and tiny bits of cornhusk over the felted carpet.

"That's going to be a pain to vacuum out. Trust me. Country dirt sticks deep," Ivy called, watching him intensely in the side mirror.

"Tell me about it. My parents will kill me if there's

dirt in this car. They inspect it weakly for scratches and cleanliness. If I get a speeding ticket or any other type of underage infraction, I've signed a contract where they not only confiscate the car, I have to repay them for the time I've had the car."

"You're joking."

"No. My parents are hardcore with their lessons on personal responsibility. I can't even let the gas tank get below ¼."

"Hey, Alex, I have an idea," Ivy beamed, her voice bouncing with excitement. "Let's go downtown."

"I don't know, Ivy. It's starting to get late, and I have some exams to study for. I think we should call it a night. I don't want my parents to get worried, and we're not really dressed to go anywhere now. You don't look like you slept in a salad bar, but you're still looking a little rough."

She laughed. She knew he was telling the truth, she saw herself in the mirror of the splash pad bathroom. Today was not her best day, but that didn't mean it had to continue to be her worst.

"I know, but your exam isn't tomorrow. And when do we act like kids? We go through all this shit, we put up with people who treat us like scum because we don't fit their idea of the perfect person, and we let people bully us." She heard Alex take a deep sigh, and saw words starting to carefully form on his lips. She didn't give him the chance to speak, though, because she knew what would come. "I know it's different, Alex. I do. I get it. I get picked on because I push people away, I challenge them, I'm rude to them, and I make myself a target. You get picked on just for existing, espe-cially around here." Her voice lowered, and she stared out the window, taking in the expanse of fields that surrounded them, hearing the peace of the quiet back roads, the birds singing, the crickets chirping, the soft rustle of the window through the large maple trees. "But, don't we have some sort of understanding? I mean, be honest with me, Alex. If you didn't at least understand why I struggle, we wouldn't be friends. You see common ground in me, even if I do it to myself. If I was just some poor trailer trash girl who was nice to everyone and people simply ignored, we wouldn't be here. We're here because you don't have to try and be anyone else with me and I might be the only one in that god awful school who slightly understands what you feel."

"It is different. But maybe you're right. Maybe we do have a small thread of understanding," he replied, somewhat disconnected, his hands running over the wood grain and leather steering wheel. "It's so stupid, isn't it? I just don't understand how people can look at someone and assume they have some sort of social or moral standing that places them above someone else. We come from the same dust, and we leave in the same dust. My parents have worked so hard to create and provide, to find their place and establish our family. But here, it doesn't matter. I'm just another ni–"

"Don't you dare, Alex," Ivy exclaimed. "Don't you dare. You can be frustrated. You can be pissed. Don't you ever downgrade who you are, what you believe in, or allow yourself to become what people try to tell you that you are. You are so smart, so talented, and you have such a big heart. If these people don't want to get to know you, or accept you, fuck them. We have two years left, Alex. Two years and then we can go anywhere. We can find our people, we can chase our dreams, we can do something. We just have to make it for two more years."

"Sounds so easy when you put it like that," he whispered. "I can't help but feel that I'm not going to see those two years, though. I don't know how to explain it. I mean, we're raised to be careful. We're raised to be obedient and submissive, mind our P's and Q's, yes Sir this, no Ma'am that, head down, no eye contact, stand your ground only when you have confidence that you have permission to do so. My life is about moving with someone else's permission.

Your life is about giving people permission. Different, yes. Similar reaction, yeah. I get it."

"How do you do it, Alex?"

"How do I not? I don't have a choice."

His words once again sat in her stomach like a heavy bag of broken up concrete, all of the jagged bits making themselves known as they ripped through her safe inner bubble of what life was meant to be.

"I guess I'm a little surprised. I've never had a bad run-in with any of our police. They've always been so kind and helpful. When we're kids, we're taught to go to them for help and to seek them out when we need them. Around here, they run into burning buildings and risk their own lives to keep our community safe. It feels like every week there's a hero fireman or policeman whose gone and done something extraordinary or started an initiative for our community. I really love our policemen," she replied, staring out the window. She was trying her best to see things from Alex's perspective, but it was so different from the comfort she knew when she saw a man in that blue suit.

"That's great, Ivy. It's great to hear someone have a positive experience. For us, though, we don't have the liberty of being raised to seek out the men who automatically assume you're a criminal because of the color of your skin. You should talk to my mom sometime. I can't tell you how many times when we were growing up that she was stopped on suspicion of shoplifting, just for being brown-skinned in a high-priced department store. And when we tell people we're from Chicago, they automatically assume we're from the south side, and we have some kind of gang affiliation," he sneered, his hands as animated as his face. The disgust, pain, and inner turmoil from the way society openly placed him and his family was obvious in the deep wrinkles forming in between his brow. "We aren't even from the south side. We had a nice penthouse condo in the Gold Coast and a house just outside of the city. And I don't dress like a thug. I make sure to not wear certain colors, I keep my shirts pressed, I keep my jeans the right size. I make sure to never put anything on that someone might look at and assume means something else. Have you ever had to do that?"

"I'm a girl. We have a fourteen-page dress code. Boys have three," she replied.

"Fair enough. But dressing for class isn't the same as knowing if you wear something you'll get arrested or shot. Have you ever had your life threatened or pulled in to a grocery store security room because you had on a red t-shirt?"

"No," she replied, her eyes firmly planted on the cornfields. She could bring herself to make eye contact with Alex. Doing so would force her to see more bits of truth about his reality, and accept that hers wasn't always standard.

"We couldn't be raised to see the police as safety. We had to be raised that these are the men who could kill us or ruin our chance for a future. I'm lucky, though. My parents did teach me to never fight back. I can remember being a little kid and we would role play different situations in the living room. Mom would pull me over or shout at me like she was a cop on a street corner, and I had to respond properly to stay alive. I was taught was to keep my eyes down, hands up and present or fingers entwined, to offer the policeman the opportunity to retrieve my wallet from my pants before reaching, and to answer everything with a sir. There would be times I would lash out and fake die. I thought it was so funny, but I didn't know the reality until I started losing my friends in high school."

"Yeah, but Alex, that's Chicago. Chicago has so much crime. I don't think you can use that as a fair example. Maybe your mom was just teaching you how to live in a city? Chicago is notorious for gangs," she scoffed.

"Chicago is also notorious for the mafia but you don't

hear about that on the nightly news now, do you? Do you really think white people don't kill each other? Have you not seen the school shootings on the news?"

"Of course I have, but those are crazy people, Alex," she replied, her voice getting louder and more heated. She turned to face him, feeling a deep resentment growing in her stomach from the way he was trying to justify the safety and comfort she felt with policemen to his fear and frustration with the exact same men. "Are you trying to act like gang violence isn't an issue? Or drugs? Look at jail. I can't believe I'm going to say this, but look at who is locked up in jail. Don't you think policemen have a right to be scared and be a little more wary of the people who kill them the most?" As the words trickled out of her mouth, she instantly felt ashamed.

"Seriously, Ivy? There's so much wrong with that. Are you saying I deserve to be stopped everywhere I go, unable to buy groceries in the wealthy areas of Chicago, or unable to walk down the street just because there are gangs on the south side? Does my mom deserve to be accused of shoplifting just because a black man shot someone on the other side of the country?"

"Well, no–"

"This one time, she went to buy a new Louis Vuitton purse. And, keep in mind, she has a huge engagement ring, diamond studs, a Rolex, and of course she's dressed nice. She went to one of the larger department stores, I can't remember which one and the girl behind the counter accused her of stealing the purse she walked in with! Why does she deserve that?"

"But it's not like that happens every day, Alex."

"No, it doesn't, but does it happen to you at all?" he shouted, one of the first times Ivy ever heard him raise his voice.

"No… No, it doesn't."

"Exactly. Even back there, you assumed you could bat

your eyelashes and walk away. You have it ingrained in you that you have an out and are above the law."

She gasped. "No, I don't."

"Really? Because I'm pretty sure you looked him in the eye and told him we were leaving, that it was a misunderstanding when he asked for our I.D. I stood in place and waited for him to give me permission to walk to the car and get my license. You absolutely think you are not only protected but that you have a right to decide when the police can enforce their rules with you."

"I... That's..." she huffed, their eyes locked together in a fierce gaze.

"Anyway," he continued. "That's just life for some people, and we have to do what we can do with what we're given... I just wish I could show people what it's like. People are jealous because my parents are rich, but they don't understand that doesn't mean anything. There was a man on the north side who got arrested in his driveway for jogging in his own neighborhood. In his own neighborhood. What was his crime? Running while black? We work hard to fit in, we talk and dress like you, we climb the ladder, and at the end of the day, I can be the son of a well educated black couple, and I'm always going to be at a lower status than a poor white girl from a trailer park." His hands sat on his head, rubbing his short hair.

"That was harsh, Alex. Is that what you think of me? That I'm just poor trailer trash and not at your level?"

"No, Ivy. That's... I'm sorry. That's not what I meant,, but that is what I said, isn't it. I wasn't referring to you directly..."

"But it's true," she said, catching her breath. "It's true. I am poor trash and – no, don't interrupt me," she said, stopping him as he inhaled to speak, wagging her finger in the air. "I get it, I do. But I don't think we should paint all cops as killers, or all black people as murderers or thieves. And maybe you shouldn't think of all white girls as privileged and above the law."

"I know. We all have to do better, but some days it feels so helpless. Some days you feel like nothing will ever change in your lifetime. I'm tired of living in the shadows and walking two steps behind. I'm sixteen, and I'm tired. I'm sixteen, and I'm scared. I'm sixteen, and I feel unequal. I'm sixteen, and every day I feel like I'm on the verge of death just for waking up."

"You've taught me so much, Alex. You have to keep hope. And, like I said before, high school is over in two years. You can leave this town, and you can go wherever you want. There have to be brighter days ahead."

"I'm sixteen, and I have to hope for better days? I'm sixteen, and I spend my days teaching people how to talk to me. Why I can't be as wild and crazy at sixteen as they want me to be. Do you know how exhausting that is? Imagine spending every day telling people how to talk to you, or why what they're saying isn't okay. I feel like a zoo animal, or like I should print a shirt that says, 'How to talk to black people: treat them like a decent human.' I'm so exhausted." His voice quaked, the crackles in his tone sending shivers down Ivy's spine. "Come to think of it, I could go for some Steak 'N Shake, and the one here is going to be super crowded right now. I really don't want to see anyone from school, and I don't want any more drama for you. I think downtown sounds like a great idea. You still in?"

"Absolutely, Alex," she replied. Her mind was full of questions she was too afraid to ask after embracing his honesty and frustrations from simply being alive. "I'm still in. Let's go live a little, even if it's just for tonight."

CHAPTER SIXTEEN

*T*he front door creaked and echoed its angry wake-up call through the dark living room, betraying Ivy's attempt to quietly enter her house. She didn't need to sneak in, but she certainly didn't want to wake her mother in case tonight was a bad night, not one of their peaceful nights. Their relationship had certainly been improving, and Ivy was starting to feel closer to her mom, almost like she was finding traces of the relationship she so desperately craved but had denied herself the right to even desire. Every hug, every pat on the back, every 'I love you' helped her to blossom a little more and more, giving her this subconscious nurturing that she wasn't even aware she needed.

"It's late, Ivy," her mother snapped, sitting up from the couch where she had been napping under the aged brown afghan. "I was worried about you. You didn't even call."

The strong concern caught her off guard, and she stumbled a bit as she took off her shoes, shocked by the dominance in her mother's voice. She had seen moments like this on TV and in movies, but she never thought she would one day be trying to quietly slide in after her imaginary curfew to a parent waiting up on the couch.

"Are you drunk?" she screeched, shooting to her feet. In a manner of seconds, her slender frame was in front of Ivy, her bony fingers wrapped around her upper arm.

"No! Geeze, Mom, that hurts. I haven't had anything to

drink – ever. I've never even tasted alcohol. I promise," she whined, trying to shake the strong claw that gripped her skin, leaving little half-moon indentations. She watched the soft red liquid start to bubble from the indentations, the slightest smell of copper drifting forward.

"Oh my goodness," her mother gasped. "I'm so sorry. I didn't mean to hurt you. Guess I better clip my nails," she nervously laughed. "Well, now that you're home, do you want to tell me about what happened today at school?"

Ivy paused. For the first time, she wondered if she should lie, if she should keep the events of the day secret, or if she did tell her mother what had taken place, how much did she need to say to her?

"Where are your clothes? Why are you wearing a boy's clothes? Oh, no. Ivy. You didn't... You haven't... That explains it. That's it. In the morning, we're going to the doctor. You're getting the pill, and you officially have a curfew. You are too young, little lady, too young!" she scolded, wagging her finger so close to her face that it brushed against the tip of her nose with soft taps.

"No, Mom. I didn't... I haven't... Ever. Trust me. I mean, I did kiss Magnus at homecoming, but that's it. And that wasn't even that good. Kind of disappointing for a first kiss. May have ruined me for men it was so bad."

"You kissed Magnus? I thought he liked boys?"

"Me, too. Turns out he likes boys and girls, but he just thought he was madly in love with me. We found out that it was misguided and untrue."

"Hmm. Makes sense, though. Well, that's a shame. He's a good kid. I like him much better than that dark-skinned boy you have coming around here. I hate not knowing if you're going to play a board game or if he's going to rob us blind." She sashayed back to the coach, slipping back under the tattered yarn blanket and gestured for Ivy to make her way over.

Ivy chose to flop into the broken recliner, careful to

hit the center of the seat before tucking her legs tightly underneath her. If she hit too far to the left, the arm would pop up and get stuck. If she hit too far to the right, the side would pop off, and she'd be forced to relocate to the couch, under her mom's feet, while the ancient recliner fell into pieces. A humorous huff escaped, recognizing this recliner as the perfect metaphor for her life. The only way she could survive and not show her broken bits was to walk down the center. Too far one way and she'd get stuck, too far the other way and she'd crumble until someone had the time to stick her pieces back together, duct taping the seams until the glue dried up and everything fell apart again.

"Your principal called today," her mother said.

Ivy didn't respond, patiently waiting for her mother to continue. This was part of the game. If she stayed silent long enough, her mom would eventually give up more information, letting Ivy know exactly what she had to reveal and what she could keep quiet.

"Did you hear me? Your principal called. He told me you got into a food fight at lunch and broke some poor girl's nose. Her parents are really wealthy, and they're threatening to sue you for bodily harm."

Shit. Ivy realized she had one option – to tell the entire story. To release every painful, embarrassing moment that proved she was a failure in the department of self-reliability. She'd have to tell her mom about homecoming, about the conversation she overheard in the haunted bathroom stall, about telling Mrs. Guinea and then yelling at Leslie, about the fight with Alex, and about that nasty group of girls and how they're set to get off the hook, successfully having blamed Ivy for their own actions.

"It's because I'm poor," she scoffed. "That's what it is. They're going to get away with this. They can attack me in the lunchroom, throw food on me, humiliate me, and when I defend myself, I'm going to be the one who pays for their sins. Is this all life is, Mom? The people on the outskirts picking up the shit for the people leaving it on the side-walk?"

"I'm not quite sure what you're asking. Why don't we start with you telling me what this is all about? Did you break a girl's nose?"

"I think so? I'm not sure. I punched her, but that's because she was about to punch me in the face with a plate full of cake after she dumped a salad, soup, and a few cans of soda on me. They had already wrecked me in front of everyone. As far as I know, I was trying to knock the cake out of her hands, and her face just so happened to get in the way."

"I hate when that happens. Well, I already asked for the lunchroom tapes, and I filed a police report for harassment. I figured since I'm the first one to file while they no doubt talk to their big shot lawyers that we may have a small lead over the competition. Let's just hope they don't conveniently lose the tapes or say something like, 'It's so odd. There weren't any tapes in the recorder during that period of lunch. This never happens! What a coincidence,'" she mocked, swinging her arms while making cartoonish expressions to match.

Ivy laughed, somewhat relieved her mom wasn't completely disavowing her story or pushing blame her way, at least not yet. "Principal Penny wouldn't even let me sit down in his office because he didn't want his chairs to get dirty. He made me stand in there and listen to those other girls lying about what happened. I was absolutely humiliated. Do you know how long it took the hall monitors to even step in and stop it? They waited until I punched Jenna in the face. They didn't care when I was sitting there having food dumped all over me and being yelled at. They only cared when one of their precious was touched."

"Well, Principal Penny said the monitors weren't in the room at the time. They had a meeting in the atrium to discuss upcoming bake sales. I know it feels like the school let you down today, but I don't think they let those girls do this to you. How did it get this bad, though? What did you do?"

"What did I do?" she growled, leaning a little too far to the left and feeling the chair start to pop and groan in complaint. "Why did I have to do anything?"

"You are my daughter. I raised you, and I know you better than anyone. Your favorite game is pushing people's buttons and then blaming them for reacting to your actions. If I am going to go into these meetings with these teachers and make sure you don't get charged with assault, I need to know everything, Ivy. I mean everything. Start from the beginning." She shifted her weight, pushing herself back up to sitting and stared Ivy in the eyes with a fierceness she hadn't seen before.

"Okay. We'll start at the beginning. Let me think of where that is, exactly, because I'm not quite sure."

She stayed silent for a few minutes, playing every moment over in her mind that stood out as challenging, painful, or less than pleasant. Rewinding through this year, she made it back to Freshman year and then the day she went from being just a quiet face in the crowd to an easy target: career fair. The day she screamed in public, cried in public, and ran out of a room full of her peers. The day she painted a sign on her back that side, "You can get to me."

Opening the wound would be painful, but now she knew she would also be ripping open the sutures for her mother. When the story began, she knew she couldn't stop, and she knew the two of them would have to proceed with caution. Taking it back to the day she was shamed for her father's death, for being blue collar, for being poor, for being working class, this would be a challenge. And, she knew that taking the events back to that point would mean she would finally need to recognize her own actions, her own chain of command, and how she reacted to the situation, thus opening her up for the events that took place earlier in the day.

Taking a deep breath, she began. Her body quivered in response to the terror she felt at being honest with her faults, her challenges, and the pain she had been fighting with since her father's death. She knew she would have to talk about their relationship, about how not having a mother figure impacted her, about how she felt like she dealt with her father's death alone, and how she was incapable of having adult friendships because she didn't know how to accept any form of relationship. Magnus was different, though, because he had always been there. And she found herself so thankful for his presence, now more than ever. She wished she could pick up the phone and call him for support, but the clock was blinking a bright 1:45 and she knew even for their friendship, that would be testing the boundaries.

"And then you and Alex skipped class," her mom said, finishing the story quietly, feeling the weight of her daughter's pain and frustration settle in. "That's a lot, Ivy. A lot. I don't know where to start. I am sorry those girls did that to you. And I'm sorry you've carried the pain of your father's death on your own. I didn't know how to get through that myself, obviously. I was so selfish to think you could do it, too. I'm going to make some tea. I don't really drink tea, but it feels like the right thing to do right now. I'll be back," she said, her voice quaking as she sprang up from the couch and padded into the kitchen, putting two mugs of hot water into the microwave.

Ivy almost informed her mother she shouldn't be microwaving the tea, but the chances of the water blowing up in her face were slim, and she felt it was best to let her mom do what she needed to do. Reflexively, she took a deep breath, feeling the frustration and pain of the last sixteen years collect itself in the very base of her lungs before shooting forward when she exhaled.

Returning with two hot ceramic mugs of tea, her

mother settled back on the couch. Ivy felt the next part of the conversation was too important to have this much distance. She carefully slid from the chair, making sure to not spill the hot tea on herself, to kick up the leg, or to push the chair to fall apart. Settling into the couch and tucking her feet under the tattered blanket, she took a deep breath in, willing her body to stay strong and to be brave.

"Can we talk about one more thing, Mom?" she shyly asked, unable to make eye contact.

"Of course. We can talk about anything. We should have been talking about anything for years, but I've really been a bad mother."

"Let's not dwell on that. I could have been a better daughter, too. But I've learned a lot this year about me, about you, about us. We need to talk about Alex," she said, finally locking eyes with her mom.

"The brown boy? Sure. What do you want to talk about?"

"Well, it's just that, Mom. We need to talk about how you talk to him...and how you talk about him. I need to be honest with you, and I need you to listen to me. I know this may be difficult for you to hear, but it's even more difficult for him, and he's my friend. He needs a safe space with me, and I need a safe space with him."

"Okay," her mother said, her lack of confidence in the direction of the conversation was blatantly obvious.

"I understand that we're from a small town. I know we don't get to meet a lot of diverse people, and what seems innocent to us, isn't always innocent to other people. A lot of things we say, like calling Alex a brown boy, or cracking jokes about him robbing our house, well, they're not funny. They're not any funnier than the rich kids cracking jokes about us being white trash or trailer trash. I need you to promise me to make a conscious effort to treat Alex like you would me, or Magnus. And I think we need to be more aware of the jokes we tell, or the way we talk to ourselves about people. We're creating a lot of negative and dangerous stereotypes in our personal conversations that impact how we look at other people. And, I know, I need to practice this with the Super Six, too. I know my attitude has given them room to treat me how they do, but I don't want to give people the power to treat me that way anymore, and I don't want to take power away from people, either. Does this make sense?"

"Somewhat. I don't think I need to censor myself, and I think some people need to grow a tougher skin. I mean, they're just jokes," she said, sipping loudly from her tea and cringing when the hot liquid made it's way down her esophagus, burning the thin flesh on its way down.

"I thought that, too. But some jokes aren't just jokes, and they're really painful. I think what I've learned is that when someone tells me my actions or words hurt them, I need to listen. I don't get to tell someone else that what I'm saying doesn't hurt them. I have to listen and try to do better with them. It's brave of them to even tell me that I'm out of line."

"I guess I can understand that. But some people are offended by everything. What am I supposed to do? Just not talk at all? It's my right to have my voice. First Amendment."

Ivy sighed, took a deep breath and willed herself to be strong. She was still new to this herself. There were lines and boundaries she didn't know how to approach, talk about, or that she didn't understand herself. "I know, Mom. Some people will be offended by everything, just like some people offend with everything. Can we at least try to start with our inner circle? Maybe I can invite Alex over this weekend. We can have pizza, and you can get to know him. He talked to me and still talks to me, about some of my issues. I didn't realize I was saying some really hurtful things," she said, her eyes downcast as she remembered the joke she first cracked in Chemistry class. "I'm still learning, too, but I can't let you hurt my friends. It's my job to teach you since I also care about you. We're a team, yeah?"

"Yes, Ivy. We're a team. If this means that much to you, bring the kid over. I'll talk to him. And, this is a new year for us. This is a new year for me to be better and if this means that much to you, or is such a big deal, I'll work on it."

"Thanks, Mom. That's all I wanted to hear." She lifted her mom's cup of tea, setting their two still steaming hot mugs on the ground, and fell into her mother's arms. She hugged her tight, nestling in and taking a minute to start making up for all of the missed hugs and moments of affection. "I'm sorry if I scared you tonight by being late. I'll make sure to call you if I am out past ten in the future, okay?"

"Thank you," her mom replied, laying a soft kiss on her forehead. "You're all I have left, Ivy. Don't leave me alone. You've just started to help me come back, and I like starting to be alive again. Don't break what little heart I have left."

CHAPTER EIGHTEEN

"**M**agnus," Ivy screamed, her voice bouncing off the fragile pre-fabricated walls of the trailer. "Get in here!"

"I'm kind of busy," he called from the bathroom, obviously annoyed.

"Well, hurry up. Leticia is about to give a press conference, and I don't think you're going to want to miss this."

She heard him mumbling and shuffling, frantically scrambling. "I'll be right there… I hope," he called.

Ivy stared at Leticia. Even after the trauma and emotional stress of the past thirty-six hours, she looked impeccable. If you didn't know her in person, you wouldn't see the subtle stress lines around the corners of her eyes, the slightly swollen pockets just underneath, the very subtle frizz popping out from her braids, or the dryness of her lips that was causing her lipstick to slip. To anyone else, she would look immaculate, and she was, but Ivy saw the signs indicating the realities of her pain.

The camera panned out to show the wide swath of reporters standing outside of their garage. The sheer number of local and national outlets was awe-inspiring, and Ivy hoped this helped get the real story out. Those hopes faded when the camera switched to ones located just at the edge of their driveway, showing a mob of picketers. They were toting signs of every color in the rainbow, scribbled with signs saying drugs weren't allowed in this neighborhood, the riff-raff needed out, links to online petitions requesting the family move, and more that she couldn't believe she was looking at.

"How appalling! Someone should go bulldoze those vultures," she sighed, unable to even cry anymore. Her body was void of emotion; even her mind felt numb.

Leticia tapped her note cards on the podium and steadied the microphone in front of her steady frame. "Hello. My name is Dr. Leticia Trowler. I am the mother of Alex Trowler. I know it's become commonplace to have these press conferences, where family members stand up and proclaim the innocence of those they lost and blame the establishment. I want to start off by saying what has happened is in no way a reflection of the entire establishment, but very much a reflection of what many of us with young black children fear.

"Alex was a great son. He was a star basketball player, like his father, Demetrius Trowler. He was an excellent student, like me, his mother, an award-winning Neuro Surgeon. I bring up our occupations to squash the rumors going around that we didn't raise him properly, that we didn't encourage him to study or to respect the law. As a matter of fact, from the time he was a child, we role-played how we should behave if he were approached by police. I would be interested in the officer from yesterday's earlier event coming forward to speak to his demeanor, but he has yet to talk about the alleged criminal behavior my son took part in previously in the evening.

"I know everyone proclaims their child is innocent, and I'm here to tell you that my son, Alex, was without a doubt innocent. Not only can I tell you this, but I can also prove this to you. What the police do not know is that we are a bit overprotective. We do weekly inspections of Alex's car, and a fleck of dirt meant we would take control of his vehicle. A dent? He would be grounded, and trust me, we would know. Some of you might say that dent happened earlier in the day when he was allegedly shooting a victim that hasn't been named, or proven to even exist, somewhere on the city's east side.

"I know, without a shadow of a doubt, these claims are fabricated to cover the tracks of an officer who got scared by a young black boy, assumed he was running drugs after he pulled out of a trailer park in a car worth more than his yearly salary, and assumed he was a dangerous man when he saw the color of his skin. I know something the police don' t know. Inside of Alex's car, there were three cameras hooked up to our private server. These cameras automatically uploaded video anytime the car was turned on. We did this for his safety, and for our peace of mind. I think anyone who is a parent of a teenager can attest to the fact that even the best-raised children still have moments of wild and careless inhibitions. If something did happen and Alex was responsible, we wanted to know. Or, if he was drinking, smoking, or being irresponsible behind the wheel, we would take proper parental action.

"If you want to view the camera video from the day in question in its full entirety, you can go to www.themurdero-fAlex.com. It's up and available, right now. Like yesterday's conference led by the commissioner, I'm sure many people are now logging on to watch the footage I've uploaded. If you're watching it, or if you're here with me wondering what's on the video, I'm going to walk you through Alex's last day alive.

"At 7:00 a.m., he left for school, where he parked in the middle of the high school's rear parking lot. The cameras stay on for two minutes after the car shuts off. You will clearly see my son walk into school. The next time the cameras come on, you will see and hear my son and the other student in question. Ivy Adams was one of his best friends, a classmate, and someone I've come to know very well. Yes, she was involved in a violent altercation at school that day. But what the commissioner left out was that she was viciously attacked at lunch, harassed, assaulted, and after sitting still for minutes waiting for a member of the school to come to her aid, reacted in self-defense and punched the girl attacking her.

"After this incident, rumors spread, and Alex was concerned about his friend. Yes, he cut class to make sure his friend was okay. He found her, in the school hallways, ninety minutes later, still covered in a variety of food and liquid the girls had dumped on her, and still in the same ruined clothes because the school refused her the opportunity to even change her clothes or wipe herself dry. My son took his friend from the school that failed her, failed them both, and knowing they would get in trouble for skipping class if they went to either of their homes, he got the bright idea to take her to the splash park.

"At this point in the video, they should be at the splash pad, and surely you've heard their conversation. Yes, we would have found out about their adventure, but we likely would have gone easy on him – easier than if he had come home during school hours. What you'll be seeing on the footage now is the other student rinsing off the dried food, and then as kids do when they're having fun, they proceed to splash, laugh, and enjoy themselves. Was this proper? No. Was it criminal? According to the rules of the park, no. According to the mother sitting on the bench who was offended and called the police? Yes.

"Now, you should be watching the entrance of the officer called to investigate the alleged criminal activity. The video is still running because the car is still on. You'll be able to hear their interaction with the officer, and even how my now deceased son urged his friend to follow all given instructions. As I've said before, we've been over these scenarios with him multiple times from childhood.

"What you'll notice is Alex left the school too late to get to any drug house or drug bust on the east side, he never fired at anyone or murdered anyone on that day. He instead took care of one of his closest friends and, as you hear now if you're watching the video, had an incredibly in-depth conversation about his fears and the reality of living as a black teenager – the very fears that came true later that night.

"The next two hours are visible, but you'll notice I sped them up to save time. You'll see the kids do go downtown, drive around the circle, sing at the top of their lungs, talk like friends do, stop in a parking garage where they go to Steak 'N Shake according to his credit card receipts and the car conversation. Next, he drives Ivy home, to the trailer park where she lives. The trailer park, where if you look at public records, has never had a single drug-related arrest and yet the commissioner made you believe it was a drug playground, giving a reason for the officer in question to follow my son when he left.

"We will watch Alex drive home, you'll see him pull in to our neighborhood and slow down to speed, and you'll watch him pull over immediately upon the officer flashing his lights. I'm convinced the officer waited until that moment because he would have no grounds to pull Alex over once he pulled in to his own address. Yes, Alex was shot directly in front of our house, at the foot of our driveway. And yes, as those of you watching the footage know by now, he called me via the hands-free Bluetooth immediately upon noticing he was being followed by a police car.

"Yes. I was on the phone with my son when he was shot. I heard him die. I listened to the shots in my house, and I knew that I couldn't run out to hold my son in his final moments because I would put myself at risk. I heard the backup officers arrive, and as you'll soon hear, you'll notice they discuss the lack of scratch and lack of dent in the car, that this model isn't the appropriate year or model, and that Officer Maxwell admits he thought the car was stolen, even though the car was coming to its registered address.

"So, while other press conferences feature stories and

anecdotes about their family members, why they were incapable of committing crimes they were accused of, or why the accused actions fall out of their known behavior for the deceased, that's not this press conference. I'm here to deliver the facts and the truth, and I've done that with the three camera views complete with audio tracks. I'm not here to convince you my son is anything you may think he is after the news took the memory of a dead child and slandered it to fit a narrative. Reports were made on the news before a single reporter came to me. Rumors were spread about the character of my son, my son that I am about to lay to rest, to avoid facing responsibility for their mistake. A mistake that ended a very promising life because it's easier to believe a young black man in an expensive car is a thug instead of a caring student who was on his way home."

"Excuse me, Mrs. Trowler," one of the reporters cut in. "I'm sorry to interrupt, and I empathize with your loss. We're getting reports that the website you stated, www.themurderofAlex.com, is unavailable and reporting an error."

"I was afraid of that," she replied, her voice showing only a slight tremble. "This is why I uploaded the videos to multiple YouTube channels and in this envelope are a copy of all three videos on individual USB sticks for each of you," she continued, holding up a translucent envelope full of thumb drives. "Because when I should be mourning my son and making arrangements, I had to defend him and relive that moment over, and over, and over again. I had to sit at a computer and transfer the data over, and over, and over again.

"You can try to silence me, but you will not stop me. I will not be silenced. I will not be stopped. Alex may have been stopped, but his memory will not be silenced. You can stand behind your uniforms and the blind loyalty of those who support you without question. You can stand behind the polished image of this town, the reputation of the school, and the fact that we don't fit in here as evidenced by my dead son and the people, at the end of my driveway, who have bought in to your lies and are wishing us dead, calling us drug dealers, and starting petitions trying to force us to move from the home that we own. You can stand behind all of this, but you will not stop me, and you will not silence my son.

"Reporters, you are free to pick up your thumb drive, but there will be no more questions. Thank you for your time today, and I kindly ask that at this time, you respect my need to mourn the death of my child and prepare his funeral. Please leave our property. And, officers, if you want to do something other than murder my child, you can come to my house and get those assholes at the end of my driveway to go home. Thank you."

Ivy watched her walk away with her head held high, noticing only the slightest twitch in her shoulders when she took a deep breath to release the tension and strength she had so effortlessly displayed in the face of tragedy.

"Should I go see her?" Ivy asked Magnus. "I feel like I should go see her, but I'm not sure I'd be able to..."

"When the time is right, then go. She'll understand. She may need her own space, too," Magnus replied.

CHAPTER NINETEEN

*T*he past week bordered somewhere between pure hell and utter devastation for Ivy. After a series of anonymous death threats had been sent, the school agreed to give her an indefinite amount of time off for healing, mental health, and to hopefully come to terms with the loss of Alex. Luckily, she didn't have to take the death threats too seriously. While they were sent via post with no signature or return email, they were sent on extremely unique custom stationery that the office recognized from when Jenna Caldwell filed her assault complaint. Needless to say, the assault charges were suddenly dropped without explanation.

For the first few days after Leticia's brave and earth-shattering press conference, a few news vans and reporters trickled into the broken down streets of Friendly Village Trailer Park, but for the most part, they left her alone. The story wasn't with her, or how they tried to frame Alex as a habitual offender through her, and for that, she was thankful. The story needed to rest within the truth for Alex, and she knew that if the reporters did come to her, she probably wouldn't help Leticia's cause. She knew herself better than anyone, and with a penchant for bottling up all emotions until she blew like Old Faithful whereupon she spouted off without end, she feared she would make the situation much worse and potentially prove their point that she was a bad influence, was complicit in the alleged crimes, and quite possibly, influenced the once talented and promising star athlete to go into a path of debauchery. That was how her brain worked, and if Leticia hadn't stepped forward with the confidence of someone who couldn't fail, even when approaching a formidable enemy, Ivy was left to wonder about all of the ways she would have driven the investigation to further implicate Alex in a myriad of crimes.

Three quick raps on the door announced the arrival of Magnus. She loudly grunted to issue permission to enter, hoping he heard her ogre calls through the frail door. The subtle screech of rusted hinges and soft scuff of the door's rough underbelly pulling on the flattened carpet trumpeted his entrance. Ivy simply grunted again, a little softer, to welcome him inside.

"Brought your homework," he said, void of energy, dropping the brown paper grocery bag on the floor with a percussive thunk.

She grunted in return, eyeing the bag and wondering how long she could get away with not doing homework as well. The school placed her on suicide watch, telling Magnus and her mother to call them immediately if they saw any signs. Suicide was not in her plans, never had been, but not because she was mentally stable. Truthfully, she was too chicken, and she knew it. Despite being angry with the world, she still felt like she had something to prove, something to become, expectations to break, and people to amaze. When the school placed the watch, she instantly felt offended. Even after years of visits to guidance counselors in her younger years, and eighteen months under the care of Mrs. Guinea, the fact that they didn't know her at all was painfully obvious. She eagerly took every private career examination test, asked continuously about school options that weren't the local community college, and tried to show interest in breaking the societal bonds on her life. Apparently, they didn't notice her eagerness to live and would always associate her health and well-being with the power others held over her. She supposed that was the curse of having low self-esteem and obvious dependency issues. Those dependency issues and habit of latching on to the slightest friendship to hold it as a rare diamond had led to Alex's death.

"You would not believe the circus that is still going on," Magnus said. "You know how they're having protests downtown to push for a federal investigation and restructure the department?"

"Of course," she croaked.

"Here, drink some water," Magnus replied, tilting a shiny aluminum tube into her hands. "They've been hosting after school 'clubs' to decorate posters and organizing carpools. The Super Six have been chatting about what they're going to wear, coordinating outfits, and even discussing the proper makeup in case they're on camera. I mean, don't get me wrong. I'm super happy that they're at least going and showing up. But they're turning it into a fashion show, or an opportunity to be seen."

"Are you chastising me for not going, Mag? What exactly do you mean by, 'at least they're going and showing up,'" she snarled, sitting up and giving the couch a moment to breathe, the cushions slowly expanding from where her body had created a seemingly permanent indention.

"Stop being so damn defensive. You're not the only one going through this," Magnus replied, none too friendly. "No, I take that back. You know what? Yes. Perhaps I am chastising you. You say he was one of your best friends. You say you are overwhelmed with thoughts that you directly led to his death, and you have the opportunity to be one of the strongest voices in this protest since they tried to use you, and yet...you're here. You're silent."

"Real nice, Mag. Real nice.," she barked. "You know what? You don't know what I'm going through. You don't have the slightest clue. Maybe I'm terrified to be targeted?

Maybe I'm afraid they'll ruin my life? Maybe they'll conveniently kill me, too. And maybe I don't want my face and my words plastered all over the world for people to send me more anonymous letters, telling me that it should have been me, or people should still come for, or that they'll kill me themselves," she shouted, springing to her feet. The floors creaked under the overstated animations as she threw around her arms, stomped her feet, and huffed so harshly she could have started a Nor'easter.

Magnus softly pressed his hands into his quads, pushing himself to his feet. "You have a take-home essay test created just for you in your English class, you're allowed to use your book for your Chemistry mid-term, and other teachers have waived your tests altogether. You'll find a full list in the front of your student planner. And maybe you should arrange for another errand boy, Ivy. I don't have time to run around and collect all of your papers. Maybe I don't want to be accused of cheating, or maybe I don't want them to think I'm doing your work, or even worse, maybe I don't want them to accuse me of not bringing any of it to you when you continue to avoid doing any work."

"That's how it's going to be? You're seriously mocking me? My concerns are valid, Magnus. You're ridiculous. Fine. I'll find my own way. I don't need you now, and I've never needed you before."

"Sure, Ivy. See, that's the problem with you. You're not downtown because you're scared. You're making excuses because it's easier to sit in this dark room like a slug than it is to go out and fight for something. You're acting like the possibility for something to happen outweighs what has happened. Let me put it this way: You're not advocating for the death of your friend because you're somehow making this all about you. Alex's death is not the Ivy show. Grieve, feel pain, examine the situation, but grow the fuck up. One of these days, you're going to realize that you had the opportunity to help him after all of the times he helped you, to show him you heard everything you two talked about, and you decided not to because your life is driven by fear. Well, I'm not afraid. I'm going and if you don't, well, whatever," he said, turning towards the door and walking out to a chorus of grunts, groans, and stammers that he gracefully ignored, answering the muted objections with a simple slamming of the door.

Aggressively returning to the couch, a string of curses flying off of her tongue every which way but Sunday, she threw the aluminum cone across the room, cringing when it hit the kitchen linoleum and slowly rolled to a loud, clanging stop.

"That's enough," her mother called, sliding her chair back with a loud and furious screech. She snapped up the now dented bottle and marched into the living room. "Enough, Ivy. Enough. I know you're hurting, I know you're grieving, but life goes on. The world goes on. And frankly, I am a little disappointed in you that you're choosing to sit here on this couch, cowering in your excuses, instead of going to stand up for your friend."

"Oh, you too? Fantastic. The two people who are supposed to keep me from suicide are now driving me towards it," she yelled.

No. Nope. I do not accept that. You do not get to blame your actions on Magnus or on me. Your emotions are your emotions, young lady. You need to deal with them and stop projecting."

"Well, I wonder where I learned that from. I had a fantastic example for eleven years of my life. Go ahead, tell me how ungrateful I am and how you're older, so you just automatically know better."

"You better watch your tongue, Ivy. I know I wasn't a perfect mother, but you don't know what it's like to lose your partner and then be stuck raising a child on your own with no plan."

"Stuck with me? That's what you think? Do you think

I killed Dad somewhere in your twisted mind? You didn't even like Alex," she screamed. "You thought he was going to rob us just because he was black. You constantly made little jokes and jabs to him. Don't even act like this effects you in any way."

"It affects me because it affects you, and one day, you'll have children and understand. Until that day, this is my house, these are my rules, and you will not speak to me with that tone or with that disrespect."

"Oh, finally, someone decides to show up and start being a mother," she spat, jumping to her feet and racing down the hallway. She slammed her door, watching the thin wall shake under the powerful reverberations, threatening to give way from exhaustion and lack of care. "I don't need any of them. None of them. I'm going to show them. I'm going to do this on my own. I'm going to prove everyone wrong. I don't need to prove myself to the school, to Mom, to Magnus, and I sure as hell don't have to prove myself to Alex's memory just because other people think it's the right thing to do."

She whipped open her laptop, feeling anger course when the aging second-hand computer whirred to life, the fan furiously spinning and vibrating the console. She would never know how it felt to have a new computer, or new clothes, or a decent meal, or a car, or even a college educa-tion unless she did it for herself and learned to provide for her own needs. "Thanks for showing me that I can count on no one, Alex," she said to the empty room, hoping he could hear her from whatever dimension, spiritual place, or metaphysical location he currently occupied. "If ghosts could exist, I wish now was the time you'd show yourself. I could use you to tell me what to do next," she whispered.

The Wi-Fi bar popped up, attempting to connect, and failing. "That can't be right," she groaned. "I need to figure out how I'm going to get out of here." She clicked on the link to connect again and patiently waited. Nothing. "Okay, run diagnostics," she replied, slapping the silver rectangular button. The verdict returned that the modem was not able to be connected to and to reset the router. "It's always something in this shithole."

She quietly opened her door, sticking her head through the crack to make sure the hallway was clear, and then tiptoed to the hall closet to check the modem. "You have got to be kidding me," she screamed. The modem was there, but the cables were not. The small black box was on its own, dead, no lights blinking to celebrate its ability to connect users to the rest of the world in seconds. "Mom," she screamed. "The router cables are missing!"

A soft chuckle drifted down the hallway, leaking from the back she stared at on the couch. "My internet, my use. I pay for it, and if you want to think you can count on no one else in your life, then start counting on no one else in your life."

"Oh, that's petty, Mom. That's really petty."

"No, Ivy. That's life. You want to blame everyone else and refuse to see even the smallest of blessings that people work hard for and share with you. You haven't once told Magnus, "Thank you," for bringing your homework, or even offered him a drink when he came in. You haven't made any attempt to reach out to Alex's parents, even though Leticia defended you on national television for God knows what reason. I'm done playing these games, and I'm done coddling your victim complex. The world is hard. No one owes you anything. Not the school, not Magnus, not me, and not Alex."

"As you wish," she replied, hearing her mother's deep sigh of non-approval and watching the judgmental roll of her eyes. Her breath hitched and for the first time in her short life that she felt was already extensive, her brain caught up to her tongue and didn't allow any of the cruel words her tongue was threatening to spill forth. The devious, self-satisfying smile that she rarely felt crept over her face as her back turned and she purposefully moved back down the hallway into the confines of her bedroom.

She knew her mother would be canceling her cell phone shortly, and she had one call she had to make.

Spiteful bitch," she sneered, harshly tapping the numbers one by one that would connect her call. "Hello, Mrs.Trowler? Leticia?"

"Hello Ivy," she said, gently and with a slight hint of relief. "It's nice to finally hear your voice."

"Can I come over? Is it safe?" she sputtered.

"Of course it's safe. It's my house, Child."

CHAPTER TWENTY

A shudder ran down her spine in perfect timing with the hollow chimes that once brought a sense of wonderment. Now, however, they filled her soul with dread, sounding fit for a funeral parlor or a large ceremonial hall where someone is about to be sentenced to death and thrown through a hole in the floor. She heard the familiar even toned clacking of sturdy stilettos, noting that even her most expensive pair didn't click over surfaces due to their low-quality materials and high percentage of questionably cheap rubber.

She expected Letitia to open the door, great her with a hug, and welcome her inside like a long lost child. But the air between them had a subtle chill and a thickness that traveled with a sudden shock down her spine.

"Come in," Letitia said, opening the door and fanning her arm. "Would you like something to drink?"

"Just some water, please, and thank you. That walk was long."

"You walked here? Why didn't you have Magnus bring you? Frankly, I'm a little surprised he isn't here, too. We'll just go into the breakfast bar. The lighting is good at this time of the day, and I think we both could use a little light."

"Magnus is heading downtown. He's convinced that's where his fight is. And, I think he feels a little cursed. This house holds a lot of death for him. I'm not sure he would be able to make it back," she said.

"Oh, really? He's already come to see me twice. He brought me those beautiful roses, right there, actually," she said, pointing towards long-stemmed yellow buds, just beginning to blossom, sitting atop the built-in desk that cornered the outer edges of the kitchen. "Did you know you can grow a rose plant from a stem? Yellow roses are a sign of friendship, actually. Very thoughtful, that one."

"Oh, I'm...I...I didn't bring anything. I'm so sorry."

"Relax, child. I didn't expect you to bring me anything, nor is anything needed. These are tough times and not the time to be worried about simple social constructs such as gifts."

Ivy wasn't quite sure what she meant by social constructs, or if there was an emphasis on the concept of a gift, and she wasn't sure if she should feel offended or relieved. With each passing day, the world became more confusing. There was this lie adults taught teenagers, that as you got older, you somehow became wiser, all-knowing, a definitive authority on life and life choices. She certainly felt older than she did last year, but the wisdom promised on the edge of the cynical responses adults constantly flung towards her to show authority was yet to appear.

Leticia placed a sparkling crystal tumbler with lemon zest ice cubes and a few fresh slices of cucumber in front of the girl who sat at her table, looking like a stray barn cat.

"Fancy," Ivy responded, clinking the cubes against the chiseled glass with each swirl of the liquid.

"Lemon will energize you. Cucumber will clean you. You should always feed your body with purpose, even if it's thirst. Feed each molecule, atom, and cell that feeds you."

Her mind swirled to her daily meals, and she wondered how many chemicals now made up her interior map. She realized that if this thought was true, there might be the possibility that her body was chemically imbalanced or possibly angry with her, thus feeding her constant need to lash out and be angry with everything that moved.

"How are you doing?" Leticia asked, her arms spread wide, hands tight on the countertop, eyes downcast.

"Not very good. It's been a bad week. I had some death threats. I'm afraid to go back to school, and I'm afraid the police will try to make an example out of me to save their butts. It's hard… I've never felt this way before."

"It's hard. Isn't it? To know you should feel one way, to have society tell you that you should believe one way, and to have to question everything you are doing before you even know you're thinking about doing it."

"Yeah," Ivy whispered. "It is." She paused, raking her eyes over Leticia, admiring her natural beauty and easy elegance. Even standing behind the kitchen counter, she looked like she just stepped out of a magazine spread. "I went to the funeral."

"I know. I saw you in the doorway," she answered, finally lifting her eyes from the countertop.

"I couldn't make myself move, though. I couldn't get myself to walk through the door. I saw you. I saw the back of your head. And I saw everyone shaking hands with Principal Penny, giving him condolences instead of you. I was livid."

"Don't be. I asked him to take that position. I don't know the children or the parents in this community. This was a tragedy, and I don't know how different people would be impacted. Principal Penny does. He'd know the different needs of people, how to talk to parents, and this gave me the opportunity for the first time in days to sit, see my baby one last time, and begin to grieve," she replied, softly lifting her chin towards the ceiling with a deep sigh, a single tear quickly wove a path down her cheek that glimmered in the soft kitchen lighting.

"Oh. But the Super Six up front were totally unnecessary. They really annoyed me. They didn't belong in the front row next to you."

"And why not? They were Alex's friends, too. They spent as much time with him as you did: class, practice, games, events. I know what happened at school. And I don't agree with that, Ivy. That's not what I'm saying. Kids can be nasty, and I know you all have some beef in there. I'm not worried about that mess. They were Alex's friends. That's what I saw when they came in and sat next to us. They sat next to us when no one else would, when other people were scared to, and when people purposely walked around us just to avoid contact because they didn't know what to say. People came to the funeral to tell me I shouldn't have said my peace, released my video, that I should have let it go." Her voice hitched and grew strong with frustration. "At my own son's funeral, people came to tell me he didn't deserve the truth," she choked, maintaining steady eye contact.

"I'm sorry," Ivy softly whispered. "For all of this. For everything."

"He made choices, too. He went downtown knowing it's out of his boundaries. He stayed out after curfew. He skipped class. Ivy, why did you come today?"

The frankness of the question caught her off guard. She found herself unable to answer, unsure of how to deconstruct the many layers posed by this seemingly simple question. Her brained furiously beat against the confines of her skull, screaming for answers that it couldn't find for itself.

"It just felt like time," she replied, her voice wavering and betraying her confidence in her answer.

"Time for what? To face your guilt?" she asked, staring Ivy in the eyes.

"Yes," she stammered.

"Child, this is not my job." Ivy looked at her quizzically, slightly taken aback by the comment. Without breaking eye contact, she continued, "You're here for forgiveness? For my blessing or to be told it's okay and it's not your fault? That's not my job. That can only come from within you, when you're truly ready to find the answers for yourself. Your pain is not my burden. Your baggage is not my burden. Your guilt is not my burden."

"But... I thought..."

"That's the problem. You think too damn much instead of acting and progressing in your life. You expect others to know what you're thinking when you don't even know. You expect to ask questions and have others do your heavy lifting, or walk behind you as your teacher. You refuse to teach yourself. I love you, girl, I really do. I've enjoyed getting to know you and see you grow, but your growth has come at a cost to a lot of people, not just Alex. Not just this situation. There has to come a day when you quit running around like a bull in a China shop. I'm not even sorry to be the one to tell you since no one else wants to step up to the plate."

Ivy sat on the tall stool with the scrolled iron back and the ornately upholstered seat, running her thumbs over the silky fabric, feeling the subtle texture of the floral weave with each pass. She had so many words she wanted to shout back, but they refused to surface.

"I never asked anyone to be my teacher or carry my burdens. I carry my own, and I carry them well," she replied, her self-belief erased and her words tinged with doubt.

"That will always be your answer until you become aware of your actions. One day, child. One day you'll understand. Is there anything else that you need today?" she asked.

Ivy understood the message. Her time was up. "No. That's all," she replied. Her quiet voice could barely be heard over the scooting of the chair's feet on the expensive Italian tiles. She didn't wait for Leticia to direct her to the front door. Stepping outside into the fresh air, she didn't have to look over her shoulder to know she was alone. The elegant clack of the expensive stilettos had not followed her to the door.

CHAPTER TWENTY-ONE

Bodies slowly filtered into the stadium-style lecture hall, chatter bouncing around the room, eyes scanning her closely. Ivy did her best to deflect the judgmental glances. She understood why her fellow students stared, whispered, and snickered as they moved past and took their seats, and she also understood it wasn't her place to question or engage. Not yet. Graduation was six years ago, yet finally taking steps to enter college was like entering high school for the first time all over again.

"Welcome to Anthropology 202: African American History and Modern Relations. I'm Professor Girard, and it is my pleasure to stand up here before you today and move you towards a better understanding of your history, your culture, or a part of American culture you are not familiar with – that's for the few white folks out in the stands," he said to almost unanimous laughter. "Many students take this class as an elective, thinking the course work will be easy, what they already know, filler work per se. I'm here to tell you this course is anything but, and if you're looking for something easy, you've come to the wrong class. I am going to challenge you, push your minds, push your own stereo-types and misguided information learned at home. By the last day of class, I hope everyone sitting in this room leaves with a fresh outlook. But don't get me wrong – fresh doesn't have to mean sunshine and rainbows. Fresh might mean you have a cause to fight for, or action to take, or it might mean you found some answers and peace. Your journey is up to you.

"Now, you all signed off on getting the syllabus last week, which means you should all know today you were to have a one-page paper prepared about why you wanted to take this class and what you hope to learn." Papers shuffled and rustled throughout the auditorium from students eagerly pulling their assignment out of binders and two pocket folders. "What you don't know is that you aren't turning this in, but you're going to present these to the class today. Taking this journey into history is something we need to do together, and to do this effectively, we need to know why each one of you currently sits in this room."

Ivy felt eyes burning into the back of her head and saw slight elbow jabs between some students around her as they nodded in her direction. Insecurity boiled inside, and she reminded herself to stay calm, even though she wished she had lied while writing her paper. She didn't know any of these people, and she didn't want to lay herself bare to them. Telling the professor in a homework assignment was one thing – telling a group of her potential peers with the right to judge her was another.

"Now," Professor Girard continued, "we'll get started. I know some of you are eager to present, but to keep this easy and help me learn you, we're going to go down the list alphabetically. Ivy Adams," he called. "Where are you?"

"He...here," she stuttered.

"The Price is Right! Come on down," he chimed with the glory of a game show host.

Ivy felt her knees knocking and her hands shaking as she walked down the stepped aisle way to the front of the room. She took her place at the podium, adjusted the microphone and looked at the room full of her fellow students, many eagerly awaiting what she had to say, already feeling they knew her reasons for being in the class.

"My name is Ivy Adams," she began. "I am a Freshman...a late Freshman because I'm just getting started in college... and I'm studying Psychology. I have a passion for finding out why people act the way they do, believe what they do, and react the way they do. I also want to help people become better versions of their selves. But, that's not exactly why I'm taking this class," her voice shook, and she bit her lip, bracing her hands on the platform and willing herself to start reading her paper.

"I am from a small town. I don't want to tell you where, but when I finish, you may know. Up until my sophomore year of high school, I had never actually met a black person, or, African American, excuse me. Clearly, I have some knowledge to work out and verbiage to understand a little better. Anyway. My sophomore year, a new kid moved to school. We were forced in to being Chemistry partners, and one of the first things I said to him was a joke about picking cotton from the acetaminophen bottle we had to open in class. He was black," she heard a gasp come from the room, "and I was ignorant and uneducated in how to talk to black people. We fought about that day for months. I hate to admit it now, but it took me a long time and many arguments to see why this wasn't a joke at all, but something emotionally harmful.

"Alex, my lab partner, became one of my closest friends, at a time when it wasn't logical for him to be one of my closest friends. I'm poor, from a trailer park, and the daughter a single, widowed mother. He was wealthy, well-educated, and his parents are a famous surgeon and ex-NBA player." She trembled, feeling the corners of her eyes moisten, spotting glimmers of recognition in the faces of some of the students. "But he saw something in me, for some reason, and he became my friend.

"Then, one day, he wasn't my friend anymore. This wasn't because he hated me, or because of a fight, but because he was shot and killed." A slight choke and gurgle slipped from her throat, but she pushed on, willing herself to get this over with and slide back to her seat where she could safely hide from the front rows of the class. "I'm sorry, I'm not going to be able to read this paper, but I'll finish up and make it quick," she said to Professor Gerard who nodded, understanding and deep interest scribbled in his furrowed brow.

"I guess it was a fight that took him from me, and I blame myself daily," she whispered into the microphone. "I don't want to get into those details, but he and I made up, he dropped me off at home – in the trailer park – and left to go back to his house. He never made it. A cop saw him pull out of my neighborhood in his expensive car and tailed him home to the gates of his mini-mansion neighborhood. The cop assumed he was a drug dealer and pulling in to the neighborhood to cause trouble. He was a black kid in a fancy car, after all. Alex was pulled over and at gunpoint, ordered out of the car. When he reached to unfasten his seatbelt, literally in front of his house, he was shot three times. They didn't call for help. Backup arrived, but they cleared the scene of evidence instead of helping him. The cop was cleared of all wrongdoing.

"I wish I could stand up here and say that I'm in this class because my friend made me an activist, or a better person, or someone who fought for your rights. But if I said that, I'd be lying. My friend made me scared, confused, and a coward. I didn't attend the marches after his death, I walked in the doors of the funeral home and then ran away, and I went back into my zone of comfort. Alex died, but my life went on as it would have had he never been in my life at all.

"This took a while for me to figure out ¬. I knew something was wrong, but I couldn't understand what, or why I felt unsettled. But realizing the why is my why for enrolling in this class." She paused before dropping her paper and looking up at the other kids in her class. "Even though I knew Alex, I can't say I know you, or your history, or what you go through every day. I can't say I understand, and I can't say that your daily life impacts me in any way. I didn't join this class to be an advocate, or to get a crown for being an ally as I've heard so many times while trying to come to terms with the pain from losing Alex, or to try and act like I'm something that I'm not. I'm just me, a person who was lucky to be born white, and even though I'm poor, has many social advantages over many of you sitting in this room. Advantages I didn't believe in, or see, or understand before Alex.

"I don't know what I'll get from this class, or who I'll be when I leave. I don't know if I'll participate frequently, or if I'll understand everything that gets said. All I know is that I want to try, and I want to hear you, and I want to try and empathize with you. I can't guarantee that after this class I'll have the strength to fight with you, and I don't even know when I have the right to fight, to speak, or to stand up with you.

"I know that me taking this class, me being here, it's very self-serving. I'm taking this class for me, and I'm not going to lie about that or try to fancy my words up to make myself seem 'woke' or anything else. I can say that I hope at the end of this semester, I have learned about challenging history, and I can think more analytically and critically about race, social interactions about race, and my potential to influence perceptions of race with those I interact with daily.

"I suppose I can say that I'm taking this class to be smarter, to be kinder, to be more aware of my actions, and to try and release some of the guilt I feel for Alex's death. And while I hope me taking this class for myself isn't selfish, I'm pretty sure that it is, because I need to get these images of one of my best friend's being senselessly murdered out of my head. I thought that if I can understand the why behind so many people's fear of a black skinned teenager in a nice neighborhood, I could maybe understand why he isn't my best friend anymore.

"I'm really only taking the first baby steps to learn, and there will be a lot of history I don't understand, or I may ask some stupid questions. And I know, trust me, I know, that it's not your job to carry my emotional educational or my emotional baggage in relation to your everyday life when I just abandoned my friend for years and went on with my life. And if you can't, I won't argue with you. But if you can, please know that I recognize all of the extra efforts you're putting in to my education.

The room was silent. Ivy's knuckles cramped from the tight grasp her fingers held on the podium for the last ten minutes of her introduction. She handed her paper over without making eye contact and walked back in silence to her chair, feeling every set of eyes trailing her movement. No one said a word, the silence only being broken by a deep sigh from Professor Gerard who hesitantly called upon the next student.

One by one, they shared their reasons for taking the class, and Ivy listened with her mind and heart open to every reason why African American history was important to her classmates. One by one, she soaked in their stories of their own confusion growing up, their own miseducation or stereotypes, and their own journey of finding their place in the world. One by one, she realized she had a hundred reasons sitting in that room to continue her journey of education.

After the closing introductory notes to finish up the introductions, Professor Gerard paused, thanking everyone for sharing, and turned his gaze to Ivy.

"We all have our own journeys, and we all have our own path to education. Our education is our burden alone to bear, but the first step is often the most powerful. I think I can speak for many when I say challenge leads to growth and for your growth, I wish you the best. To Alex," he closed, holding his hand up with a nod of his head.

Ivy sighed as the rest of the class rang out in agreement, "To Alex."

DISCUSSION QUESTIONS:

1. The first joke Ivy breaks out with Alex is introduced as one of her mother's favorites. How do jokes and stereotypes under the guise of humor help to perpetuate racism and inequality in youth?

2. Ivy's mom assumes Alex is an inner city student simply because he's a person of color, despite knowing his mother is a hotshot doctor. How do stereotypes guide our impressions of people despite having additional information about them?

3. A secondary theme in *How To Talk To Black People* is an exploration of class systems. What did you notice about how the different class systems relate to the main theme of racism and bigotry? How does class impact Alex and his journey?

4. There are a considerable amount of uncomfortable scenes in *How to Talk to Black People.* Some of these come from the author's experience in her hometown, some come from statements she saw on Facebook friend timelines, and some come from the headlines. Which one stands out the most to you and why?

5. Magnus finally tells Ivy his grandmother was a woman of color, which makes Ivy think of many challenging things she's said around him. Why do you think Magnus never spoke up to Ivy before Alex arrived?

6. If you were Magnus, would you have talked to Ivy

sooner? What responsibility do you think friends have for each other and their actions?

7. When Ivy starts to become more self-aware, she starts to become very defensive over Alex and the injustices she sees. She hasn't yet learned there's a difference between being 'woke' and overshadowing a person of color's opportunity to tell their own story or represent themselves. How do you think you can support marginalized groups in the face of adversity without taking away their agency?

8. After Alex dies, Ivy can make a choice. She can return to her life as if nothing happened, or she can continue to grow and pursue a new path full of self-awareness. What do you think about Ivy's choices? What do you think about the town's choices when faced with the same opportunity to grow and embrace the truth?

Printed in Great Britain
by Amazon

53489311R00124